S0-AVE-100

What do you look for in a guy? Charisma.
Sex appeal. Confidence. A body to die for.
Looks that stand out from the crowd. Well,
look no further—this brand-new collection has
four guys with all this—and more! And now
that they've met the women in these novels,
there is one thing on everyone's mind....

NIGHTS OF PASSION

One night is never enough!

The guys know what they want and how
they're going to get it!

Don't miss any of these hot stories, where
electrifying romance and sizzling passion are
guaranteed!

The Tycoon's Virgin
Susan Stephens

Bedded for Diamonds
Kelly Hunter

His for the Taking
Julie Cohen

Purchased for Pleasure
Nicola Marsh

Dear Reader,

Welcome to February's NIGHTS OF PASSION collection, featuring four brand-new, passionate novels. These offer more of what you love—strong, sexy alpha heroes; dramatic, sizzling, sexy story lines and a variety of exciting backdrops from around the world. In this collection, all four stories feature NIGHTS OF PASSION—*one night is never enough!*

If you love a millionaire—or a billionaire, for that matter—check out our next collection, TAKEN BY THE MILLIONAIRE, available March 2008. Find out what happens when these ordinary women enter the glamorous world of the superrich....

We'd love to hear what you think. E-mail us at Presents@hmb.co.uk or find more information about books and authors at www.iheartpresents.com.

With best wishes,

The Editors

PURCHASED FOR PLEASURE

NICOLA MARSH

NIGHTS OF PASSION

HARLEQUIN®

TORONTO • NEW YORK • LONDON
AMSTERDAM • PARIS • SYDNEY • HAMBURG
STOCKHOLM • ATHENS • TOKYO • MILAN • MADRID
PRAGUE • WARSAW • BUDAPEST • AUCKLAND

ISBN-13: 978-0-373-82070-2
ISBN-10:   0-373-82070-4

PURCHASED FOR PLEASURE

First North American Publication 2008.

www.eHarlequin.com

Printed in U.S.A.

CHAPTER ONE

THE minute Kate Hayden saw Tyler James again, her world turned upside down.

Okay, maybe nothing quite so dramatic, but it sure seemed as if her axis tilted way off kilter as the gut-wrenching desire that had been a feature of their brief relationship eons ago was back, overwhelming in its intensity.

It had been six, long years since she'd last seen him so why were her hormones going haywire at the sight of him now?

She'd gotten over him a long time ago.

She'd prepared for this.

She'd psyched herself up for weeks ever since she'd seen his name on the list of 'Odd Bods', the rather quaint name given to the charity man auction the magazine was sponsoring, and known she had to see him.

So she was curious? No big deal. She'd been nosy her whole life and the trait served her well in her job, giving her a head-start on the next big story, helping her make a name for herself.

But this insatiable curiosity about Ty was different and she'd known it the minute her tummy had tingled at the sight of his name on the auction list.

This wasn't just the natural curiosity of an investigative journalist. Uh-uh.

This was the intense burning curiosity of a woman who'd walked away from the best thing that had ever happened to her.

First loves weren't supposed to last and she'd moved on a long time ago, but somehow seeing his name on that list had brought back a rush of memories, all good, and she had to see him.

She'd hoped he'd be shrunken and balding and his muscles had wasted away. Although where would the fun be in that?

She sipped her champagne, hoping the bubbly liquid would ease the sudden dryness of her throat as the guy she'd once thought she'd spend the rest of her life with strutted across the stage.

Oh, my.

The champagne momentarily soothed her thirst but it did nothing for her erratic pulse, which skipped all over the place at the sight of the sexiest guy she'd ever met standing on display to a room full of women as if he didn't have a care in the world.

Ty looked incredible, far hotter than she remembered—and she remembered a lot! If anything, the years had enhanced his rugged good looks. Fine lines radiated from the corners of his blue eyes doing little to detract from the tanned, hard planes of his face, his high cheekbones hinting at arrogance. Rich brown hair streaked blond by the sun, cut in the traditional short-back-and-sides he favoured. And those finely shaped lips…

Oh, yeah, she remembered those lips all too well, seducing her with their skill, giving pleasure, wreaking havoc.

The memories still lingered, imprinted on her brain, branded there, utterly indelible. She'd deliberately blocked them over the years, concentrating on her career, trying to build a life for herself in a new country.

Leaving Sydney for LA had been a huge decision for a twenty-one-year-old. But meeting Ty shortly after she landed in the US had made that transition a lot less scary; in fact the guy had lit her world back then.

Squirming in her chair, she took another sip of champagne. This wasn't the time to get caught up in memories of Ty. She had to focus her attention for the next ten minutes, at least till she'd given her speech. Senior editors needed to be cool and poised, not hot and bothered while practically drooling over an old flame.

'So, without further ado, ladies, I present our last Odd Bod for the evening. Though from where I'm standing there's nothing odd about this particular bod!'

A soft twittering swept the room as all eyes turned to the stage. Kelly Adams, the glam local TV station presenter, gestured to the man on her right as she continued her spiel.

'I know you'll like what you see, ladies. Tyler James is a Navy SEAL instructor. By the way, SEAL stands for Sea, Air and Land, for those of you who don't know, and they're an amazing bunch of Special Forces guys. Tyler stands at six feet four with muscles to die for, has amazing blue eyes, is equipped to handle anything and likes to take charge!'

Catcalls and whistles filled the air while the man in question squared his broad shoulders and grinned, not in the least embarrassed.

'So, what am I bid for Tyler? Come on, ladies, dig deep. The Ramirez Orphanage is a good cause that needs your help to stay open. Besides, who wouldn't want this man doing their odd jobs for the next week? Perhaps a spot of gardening? Car washing? Cooking? Housework? Your call, ladies. I'd bid myself though I think my husband would have something to say about it. Who'll start the bidding?'

As Kelly's announcement sank in Kate pondered his change in career. Ty had become an instructor? When they'd first met he'd been a proud SEAL, resplendent in his uniform and bristling with macho ideals. No behind-the-scenes action for that guy. He'd been committed and passionate with a genuine love for his career. Why the change of heart?

She stared at the man on stage, questions swirling through her head.

Why hadn't they given it a go?

Had chasing their careers rather than following their hearts been worth it?

Had growing up changed them?

Needing a distraction from her futile questions, she glanced around the table and noticed every woman's attention riveted to the stage. Not that she could blame them, considering what was on show up there.

They were a great bunch of girls to work with, all highly talented in their own right: journalists, editors and photographers. Diane, her personal assistant, had organised this gathering in support of the magazine's sponsorship of the orphanage. In fact, Di had been in charge of choosing this year's worthy cause and had taken care of every detail and all she'd had to do was turn up.

As if sensing her gaze, Di turned towards her.

'Why don't you put in a bid, Kate? About time you had some excitement in your life.'

Excitement? Her? No way. Been there, done that and still had the SEAL scars to prove it.

To her mortification, the rest of the girls turned to look at her so she schooled her features into her best 'I'm too busy to have fun' look.

'Sorry to disappoint, everyone. No time for excitement. What would I do with an Odd Bod anyway?'

Though her voice remained steady the idea of Ty trailing after her for a week did strange things to her insides.

Things she shouldn't be feeling…or remembering…

'My point exactly,' Di smirked. 'If you don't know what to do with a total hunk like that you need more help than I first thought. Why don't you live a little and show us you're human after all?'

The rest of the table joined in, goading her into bidding and she shook her head, chuckling at their enthusiasm.

So Di had a point. She did bury her life in her work, determined to show that effort and dedication were the keys to success. However, being a workaholic had its downside and she hadn't had any fun in ages. She'd been fun and impulsive once, and she was too young to be living the sensible 'all work no play' life. Maybe a brief catch-up off-stage with an old 'friend' could be an antidote to that?

What harm could placing a bid do? It wasn't as if she'd be the only one. Just one look at Ty and every woman in the room would be reaching for their cheque books.

'Okay, okay. I'll do it. Sheesh.'

She held up her hands in surrender and grinned as the girls cheered. Downing the rest of her champagne in two gulps, she raised her hand high in the air and waved it like a cheerleader on a caffeine high.

'Five hundred dollars,' she yelled, buoyed by the alcohol and a sudden rush to do something completely out of character.

Pin-drop silence followed and rather than sinking into her chair with embarrassment she straightened her spine, head up, waiting for the moment Ty laid eyes on his bidder, eager to see his reaction, wondering if they still had a spark.

She had her answer in the next loaded second when Ty focussed that too-blue gaze of his on her, the shock of recognition registering in the imperceptible widening of his eyes across the room as they stared at each other, neither backing down, locked in an invisible battle of wills so reminiscent of the past.

Maybe it was the champagne, maybe it was the number of women packed into the room, but while Kate sat trapped under the intensity of Ty's stare she broke out in a sweat as her body temperature sky-rocketed and she could barely breathe.

'Do I have any further bids?' Kelly queried, surveying the room with a grin on her expertly made up face.

Please. Someone…anyone…

Kate's silent plea preceded complete and utter bedlam as the ladies—and she used the term loosely—in the room erupted.

Maybe her initial bid had been a tad on the high side considering the average guy had gone for around three to four hundred all night. But she'd wanted to prove a point to the girls, show them she could lighten up when needed. Unfortunately, she hadn't counted on the speculative gleam in her ex's eyes or the competitive nature of her fellow bidders.

'Five-fifty!' shouted a boppy blonde.

Kate rolled her eyes. Blondes were so not Ty's type.

'Six hundred,' yelled a willowy redhead who looked like Nicole Kidman, her smug smile indicating she thought she'd won.

'Six-fifty.'

Kate sat up and took notice of the third bidder, a sultry brunette reminiscent of Catherine Zeta-Jones with breasts that could take out a guy's eye at a hundred paces.

Now she was Ty's type.

Di leaned over and muttered behind her raised hand. 'Hey, are you going to let these amateurs beat you?'

Suddenly, Kate knew that was out of the question. Fuelled by a fierce competitive streak she'd had since birth, she downed her newly topped-up glass of champagne and jabbed her hand high in the air.

'One thousand dollars!'

Chaos ceased as curious eyes—and several eyes shooting daggers if she counted the blonde, Nicole and Catherine—focussed on her and she clenched her fists under the table, her heart pounding.

'Going once? Going twice? All done?'

As the gavel in Kelly's hand hit the podium with a resounding thud Kate jumped.

'Sold. To Kate Hayden, whose magazine is our major sponsor today. Well done, Kate. Why don't you come up here and claim your prize?'

'You go, girl,' Di laughed, slapping her on the back. 'Didn't know you had it in you.'

Numbness flooded Kate's body as she walked towards the stage mechanically putting one foot in front of the other as thunderous applause rang out, almost succeeding in drowning out the pounding of her heart, which still reverberated in her ears.

Well, wasn't this just peachy?

She'd envisaged a brief catch up with Ty tonight, but not like this. A short, impersonal meeting off-stage had been her goal, not an up-close-and-personal encounter in front of the whole room.

As she dragged her feet up the steps she looked Ty in the eye and tried not to crumple into a pathetic heap at his feet. Up close he was even more handsome if that were possible. His vivid blue eyes, the spectacular colour of the Pacific Ocean at Malibu on a fine day, had a quizzical edge as his glance raked over her, setting her body alight.

Damn, he was hot. Hotter than hot and she was burning up from the inside out just being this close to him.

'You're looking good, Katie. Long time no see.'

His deep voice flowed over her in a warm caress just as it used to and her knees wobbled, an instant reminder of her foolishness when it came to this guy.

Rattled by her reaction, she aimed for cool. 'Yeah, it has been a long time. Amazing what I'll do for charity, isn't it?'

The momentary warmth in his eyes sparked into fire, the same fire that had scorched her with its brilliance on more than one lucky occasion.

'Now, now. Is that any way to talk to your *fiancé*?'

'Ex,' she muttered, unable to keep her mouth from twitching at the teasing glint in his eyes.

Those incredible eyes…she was convinced they had the

power to make her do crazy things. Why else would she be standing here like a hypnotised chook unable to look away?

Kelly's head swivelled between them, her catlike eyes glowing with interest.

'Well, well. Seems like these two are going to get along famously. They're already chatting. Why don't you say a few words, Kate, before we wind things up?'

Kate tore her gaze away from Ty's mesmerising stare and strode to the podium, hoping that her professionalism wouldn't desert her while her mind was a useless jumble of unexpected memories.

'As senior editor for *Femme* magazine I'd like to thank you all for attending our Odd Bod Man Auction here tonight.'

Glancing at the piece of paper thrust into her hand, she continued, 'Thanks to your generosity we've raised over ten thousand dollars for the Ramirez Orphanage. Well done, ladies.'

Particularly well done to her considering she'd contributed one tenth of that money to 'purchase' the guy she had every intention of cutting loose once this evening was over. The money didn't irk nearly as much as the fact he now knew she'd outrageously overbid to beat every other woman in the room to have him, not once, but twice.

The smattering of applause died down and she forced herself to concentrate on finishing up the speech.

'I'd also like to thank the men who generously volunteered their time tonight and for the next week. I'm sure the ladies will be more than thrilled to have personal Odd Bods for the week ahead. I know I am.' *Not.*

There, that last remark should show him that he hadn't affected her. Not much, anyway.

Squaring her shoulders, she turned to Ty and flashed him an uneasy smile. Once again loud applause filled the room as he blew her a kiss.

Damn it, her knees wobbled again. All it took was one

stupid little gesture and she was acting as she had when they first met: star-struck, smitten and totally unable to control her reactions to him.

Leaning on the podium for support, she fixed a bright smile on her face and turned to the audience.

'Thank you, ladies. We hope to see you at our next fund-raiser.'

As she stepped away Kelly grabbed her arm.

'Not so fast, Kate. Have you forgotten what the last step is after a successful bid?'

Her heart plummeted. She'd been hoping to escape the final humiliation every other woman who'd purchased an Odd Bod had gone through. The goofy friendship bracelets bearing a strong resemblance to handcuffs to shackle the Odd Bods to their bidders were tacky to say the least. And it looked as if she'd have to grin and bear it.

'Come on, you two. Don't be shy. Kate, you can remove this any time you want…if you're game.'

With that final remark, Kelly snapped the bracelet onto her wrist, the other end already securely fastened to Ty's, and dropped the key into his jeans pocket.

'You've got to be kidding,' Kate muttered, silently vowing she would never drink champagne again.

Though deep down she knew it wasn't only the alcohol that had made her bid for Ty. One look into those gorgeous baby blues after all this time and she'd lost it.

Though she didn't have feelings for him any more the thought of some other woman having him trailing after them for a week performing goodness knew what duties had been incentive enough to make her commit the ultimate folly, that ludicrous bid to end all bids.

'No joke, I'm afraid. Looks like the fun's just beginning,' Ty said, swinging their bound arms into the air in a victory salute.

The applause crescendoed, accompanied by raucous hooting and laughter, and light bulbs flashed in a continuous wave as the contingent of photographers lapped up the opportunity. Kate clenched her jaw and grinned, determined to appear in control when in fact she wanted to bolt.

'Yeah, I'm having a real ball,' she said through gritted teeth, keeping her smile in place and giving a subtle yank on the chain binding them.

'Just a little longer. Plenty of time to get *reacquainted* later.'

His subtle, husky emphasis on 'reacquainted' set her pulse racing and she took a deep breath, knowing the faster they got off-stage and unlocked, the happier she'd be.

She lowered her arm forcefully, pulling his down, and Ty tugged on the chain linking them, reinforcing the fact that if he hadn't wanted to lower his arm she wouldn't have succeeded in moving him one inch.

'Let's go.'

She marched off the stage, leaving him no option but to follow.

Now was her big chance.

To do what?

Exchange pleasantries? Make small talk?

Chewing her lip in frustration, Kate picked up the pace. For someone who spent her life making decisions over which words sounded better or which articles went where, she hadn't thought this through at all.

Seeing Ty on stage was one thing, having him attached to her up close and personal another.

She'd wanted to catch up? Well, looked as if she had her opportunity considering she'd spent a small fortune to have him bound to her for a week.

Not that she'd hold him to it. They'd have a quick catch-up backstage and she'd let him go.

Yeah. That was exactly what she would do. Simple.

Then why did she feel as if fate was chuckling and the joke was on her?

Tyler shook his head. Still the same old Kate: proud, gorgeous, independent, with those bewitching hazel eyes that got him every time.

He'd enjoyed teasing her during their brief relationship, the golden flecks in her eyes sparking whenever she reacted to his banter. Those flecks had also glowed when she'd been aroused, as he remembered all too well.

He'd been floored when their gazes had locked across the room, her presence at the auction a sucker punch to the gut when he'd least expected it, and try as he might he'd found his gaze drawn to her repeatedly while she'd acted as if he didn't exist.

Then what had that crazy bidding been about?

Damned if he knew.

'Keep up,' Kate said, giving a none-too-subtle yank on the chain binding them, and he bit back a grin.

She hadn't changed at all, still the same determined woman who wasn't going to wait for anyone, as she picked up the pace.

His gaze travelled to her butt and the way the black linen skirt clung to every sexy, provocative curve. She didn't merely walk. She strutted and then some on long legs, showgirl legs, sensational legs that had wrapped around him so many sweet times.

The great thing about her height was it didn't detract from her curves one iota. In his experience, tall women were usually lean with small breasts and few curves. Kate, however, was the antithesis of this stereotype. For a woman about five-ten, her voluptuous breasts and narrow waist would put an hourglass to shame.

She was a knockout, pure and simple.

He wrenched his gaze away from her butt and his mind out

of fantasy land and focussed his attention on her hair, admiring the sleek, new style. Shorter hair suited her. The burgundy highlights in the chocolate-brown depths drew attention to the shiny mass that now brushed across her shoulders and he itched to run his fingers through it.

Unfortunately, it seemed moving his view higher hadn't dampened his growing desire. If anything, the thought of her luscious locks trickling like soft silk through his fingers inflamed him further.

Looked as if he still had it bad. No great surprise there.

How many nights had he lain awake dreaming about her, wishing he could reach out and touch her? In fact, the fantasies about Kate had been one of the few things that had kept him sane during the agonising year-long knee-rehabilitation programme two years after their split, when dreary days had merged into pain-filled nights as he had tried to come to terms with the fact his knee was bust, no amount of exercise could ever repair the damage and he'd be off Team Eight, removed from active duty permanently.

Life had sucked big-time back then.

Now, it looked as if his fantasy had come to life again. So what was he going to do about it?

From the first minute he'd caught sight of her sitting at a table surrounded by beautiful women yet standing out anyway he'd been stunned. She'd been staring at him, her luscious mouth a perfect little pout, and he'd had difficulty breathing. In fact, his first glimpse of Kate after six long years had been worse than a case of the bends, and no amount of hyperbaric chamber treatment would fix what he had for her.

Lust, pure and simple, had slammed through his body, making him want to leap over tables, grab her and lock his mouth to hers, tasting her, possessing her, reminding her of how damn good they'd been together in the bedroom.

He stumbled and she cast a pitying glance over her shoulder while he sent her a cocky grin.

Staring at his sassy ex strutting in front of him had him remembering exactly how great they'd been together. Perhaps spending seven days trying to resurrect old times before facing the life-changing appointment next week wouldn't be such a bad thing?

Yeah, that sounded like a plan.

And like any good SEAL, he always stuck to the plan.

CHAPTER TWO

KATE didn't speak till they reached the confines of a dressing room backstage. With Ty's stare boring holes into her back, it took her a while to figure out what to say.

Her plan to have a quick chat and catch up had sounded good at the time. However, now that she actually had him all to herself her plan had hit a snag. A big one.

She hadn't banked on the familiar zing between them, that special something that had prompted her to propose to him in the first place. Back then he'd thought it had been a bit of a laugh and she hadn't disillusioned him.

She'd played it down, they'd joked about being engaged, he'd attributed it to her crazy sense of humour, but deep down she'd known it hadn't been real. They were two crazy kids in love, him fresh out of SEAL training, her fresh off the plane from Sydney. Vegas had been a hoot, hooking up with the fun-loving SEAL even more so, and it had seemed natural to move in with him back in LA.

But life wasn't just about fun and they'd both had places to go, careers to pursue and they'd done the right thing in splitting up.

Hadn't they?

Kate closed the door behind them, determined to make their catch-up short and sweet. Either that or succumb to a sudden hankering for a fix of seal and it sure didn't involve going to the zoo to get it.

'Look, I know this must seem crazy to you, me bidding and all. But I just wanted to catch up. Basically, I've no intention of holding you to this odd-jobs stuff. I'll happily donate the money to the orphanage and we can call it quits, okay?'

He remained silent, a speculative gleam in his blue eyes with the barest glimmer of a smile playing about his sexy mouth.

Disconcerted by his silence and the look in his eyes, she rushed on. 'It's been a while, hasn't it? Guess I just got curious, wondering what you've been up to. Six years is a long time.'

Could she sound any more pathetic?

Standing this close to Ty, having that intense blue stare focussed solely on her, was short-circuiting her brain. Not to mention the nerve-endings firing through her body.

'It is a long time.'

His cool tone was at odds with the banked heat simmering in his eyes and she shivered despite the warmth of the room.

'So a quick catch-up before cutting you loose isn't so bad, right?'

She forced a fake laugh, expecting him to join in and agree.

'No.'

Typical Ty: short, sharp, to the point and the opposite of what she expected him to say or do.

'What?'

'I said no.'

'No, you don't want to catch up or no, you don't want to be cut loose?'

Oh-oh, why did her voice have to do that, go all soft and low and husky? As if she were baiting him? Tempting him?

It was his fault. Less than a few minutes in his company after six years and she'd fallen into flirt mode automatically.

He shook his head, a slight frown appearing between his brows, accentuating the age lines that fanned from the corners of his eyes. Though little could detract from his good looks Ty looked older, weary, as if he'd fought a thousand battles.

'I don't want a quick catch-up.'

'Oh.'

She couldn't stand this. He was confusing the heck out of her just as he'd always done by keeping his emotions under tight control while burning her up with those 'come get me' eyes.

'I want a long one. I want to hear everything you've been doing. Everything.'

His eyes darkened to the colour of her favourite stone, a deep blue sapphire, and the comparison disconcerted her. She didn't want to compare him to anything as precious as her grandma's heirloom ring.

'It's been way too long, Katie.'

His smooth, steady tone did little to placate her as she tried to ignore the way her heart thumped when he said her name in that familiar way.

'Uh-huh,' she said, wishing she could think of something witty to say rather than standing here captured in the intensity of his stare, wondering if he knew the effect he was having on her after all this time.

'So what do you want to do?'

Fling myself at you?

Tear your clothes off?

Have my way with you?

She had to think of something sensible to say, something to break the tension.

'What do you want to do?'

Rather pathetic but at least she'd put the onus firmly back on him. Let him make the decision. She couldn't think straight and control her impulse to jump him at the same time.

'This.'

His husky tone sent a shiver of anticipation skittering down her spine and before she knew what was happening he had tugged on the steel links binding them, hard.

She fell against his body, the wind knocked out of her, reaching for him to steady her as his head descended, blocking out the harsh glare from the mass of light bulbs around the mirrored walls.

Oh, wow…

His lips crushed hers, frantic, hungry, but oh-so-sweet. Her mouth burned beneath his as his kiss demanded and she gave without thought, without reason.

Pure, blind need shot through her body as she responded to him on some kind of instinctive level.

This can't be happening, flickered through her mind as his tongue nudged her mouth open, urgent, exploring, begging her to match him for pleasure. Not again.

Her stomach dropped away as his commanding kiss deepened, logic fleeing as his tongue ran along her bottom lip, driving her crazy with longing.

She'd missed this, missed him more than she'd realised, and as his teeth followed where his tongue had been, nibbling and nipping with precision, she realised the strange whimpering sounds filling the air were coming from her.

'Ty.' She whispered his name, lost in waves of electrifying sensation as her body trembled under his expert touch, currents of desire shooting every-which-way.

No other man had ever made her feel this way. Only Ty.

And it had been six, long years.

She strained against him, encountering hard evidence of how much he wanted her. Her eyes flew open and she turned her face away, staring at their reflected embrace in the mirrored walls. Reality sank in as she watched him rain kisses up her throat and she pushed him away, barely able to tear her gaze away from the mirrors. He followed her stare, a lazy smile tugging at the corners of his mouth.

'We still look good together, huh?'

His words roused her from the sensual fog that had enveloped them as reality crashed in.

What was she thinking, responding to him like this?

She was a big girl now, not some love-starved, naïve tourist who'd landed in a new country and ended up staying.

'Dream on,' she muttered, hating how she'd melted into a mushy marshmallow under his hot kiss, hating that he was right even more.

They did look good together. Too good. A picture she'd believed in six years ago before realising it was a mirage and mentally ripping it in half.

He chuckled, tracing a finger from her cheek to her jawline with torturous patience.

'Maybe I was out of line with that kiss but I think you wanted it as much as I did.'

Damn him for knowing her almost better than she knew herself.

'I'm tired. I responded without thinking.'

Yeah, and she practically melted into a heap at the feet of the nearest sexy guy whenever she was exhausted—which happened to be often considering the office hours she kept. As if.

He grinned. 'Great response. Maybe this catch-up was meant to be? Maybe your subconscious prompted you to buy me because you still want me? Maybe—'

'You're full of it,' she said, mortified by how easily he could read her, by how that one kiss had resurrected a whole host of sensual memories she'd assumed long forgotten.

The impulse to be fun and spontaneous had not been one of her brightest ideas. She'd end this now if she could get her brain to slip back into gear and her heartbeat back under control.

Ty ran his free hand through his hair, the usual short-back-and-sides that suited him so well, and for an irrational instant she had the urge to do the same.

'Insult me all you want but I'm not going anywhere. Though can we catch up some other time, maybe tomorrow? I've had one helluva week on the job and I'm beat.'

He did look tired and as a grimace of pain distorted his handsome features and his posture stiffened she wondered what he'd had to face over the last few years. When they'd first met he'd been fresh from BUD/S, the intensive training to become a SEAL, and as fit as a Mallee bull back home. Now he looked dead on his feet.

'Besides, I need some sleep if I'm to perform all those odd jobs you probably have lined up for me over the next week.'

Kate heard the teasing lilt back in his voice and sighed, ignoring his innuendo. She'd had a long week meeting killer deadlines at *Femme* and she didn't want to prolong this. Seeing Ty again had her more wound up than she'd anticipated, and as for that kiss…

'You want to go through with this? Are you insane?'

'Not like I used to be.' He grinned, the same smile that had captivated her so many times in the past. 'And, yeah, being your Odd Bod for a week could be interesting.'

Sighing, she said, 'It's not going to happen but we'll talk about this in the morning. I don't have the energy to argue with you right now. I think you're crazy, you don't, so let's agree to differ till I sort you out and we go our separate ways. Now, unlock me, please.'

'Sorry, you'll have to do it.'

'Come on, give a girl a break. No more games. Give me the key.'

His grin widened. 'I can't. In case you haven't noticed, my left hand is connected to your right and the key is in my left pocket. At the risk of dislocating my right shoulder, I think you better do the honours.'

She stared, annoyed at the twinkle in his eyes and the devilish smile, sure that he could remove the key if he really tried. However, he didn't move an inch and continued to watch her as if he was enjoying every minute of her discomfort.

'Well, what's it to be? Do you prefer being linked to me indefinitely or rummaging around my pockets and seeing what pops up?'

Ignoring his laughter, she struggled with the decision. Sink or swim time. Either way, she'd always been lousy in the water.

'You're such a child.'

Kate delved her hand quickly into his pocket; thankfully the key wasn't too deep and she didn't have to feel around. Though it could've been fun.

'Not half as childish as you.' Ty chuckled. 'I'm not the one pouting.'

She thrust the key into the lock and turned. Typical of her luck this evening, it stuck.

'I'm not pouting. Help me with this, will you?'

She jiggled the key to no avail and his chuckles turned to laughter.

'If you're not pouting you must be limbering up those lips for another kiss. They're looking rosy and full and very, very sexy.'

Her patience snapped and heat seeped into her cheeks as his smooth words recalled her attention to the crazy way she'd responded to his unexpected kiss moments before.

'Cut the suave act, sailor boy. I'm not in the mood. Let's open this damn lock so I can get out of here.'

'Here, let me try.'

As his hand enclosed hers she couldn't ignore the heat. It sizzled through her body every time he touched her, even at the innocuous touch of his hand trying to open the lock.

She'd lied. She was definitely in the mood.

'There. You're a free woman.'

I wish.

Unfortunately, seeing Ty tonight, swapping banter with

him, even getting mad at him for that presumptuous kiss had woken her up.

She wasn't as free as she'd like to think.

She might have got over him a long time ago and moved on with her life, but it hadn't taken much more than a kiss to snap her emotions back to attention and right now they were firmly focussed on the sexy SEAL.

The lock snapped open and the bracelet sprang apart, clattering to the floor at their feet, and Kate winced as her wrist freed. She'd been so engrossed in her reaction to Ty turning on the charm that she hadn't realised the hard plastic and steel had bitten into her soft flesh.

'Thanks.'

She glared at him, wishing he didn't look so darn appealing when he smiled, absent-mindedly rubbing her wrist.

'Let me do that.'

Before she could protest, he reached over and captured her wrist between his hands, slowly massaging till the circulation returned to her aching flesh.

'Mmm…that feels good,' she murmured, her eyes drooping with fatigue.

However, as the pain in her wrist eased a deeper, more demanding ache increased, an ache she'd determinedly ignored for years. His hands were warm, firm, attuned and she imagined them leaving her wrist, travelling up her arm to her tight shoulders and then sliding down the rest of her body.

'Better?'

Her eyes flew open as he relinquished her wrist and her gaze locked on his, questioning, hungry, reflecting the need she knew must be visible in her own. That all-seeing blue stare that had captured her so long ago, mesmerising her in the blink of an eye.

'Would you like a lift home?'

She shook her head, knowing the last thing she needed right now was to be holed up with him in the confines of a car.

'Thanks, but I'm fine. I came with the girls and we're headed back to the office.'

He glanced at his watch. 'We've been here a while. Maybe they've gone?'

'Don't worry about it. If they have I'll take a taxi.'

Kate knew she sounded petulant but couldn't bear being this close to him one second longer. If he took her home she'd be tempted to ask him in and, considering her reaction to his kiss, she knew exactly where that could lead.

Her sex life had been one, continuous dry spell since her last brief relationship had ended eighteen months ago and she had no intention of letting Ty be her drought breaker.

He laid a hand in the small of her back and guided her to the door. 'Let's check it out. It's no problem, really. Where do you live?'

'Beverly Hills.'

'Pretty impressive.' He looked at her with admiration and pride filled her.

'My grandparents built the place. We hooked up after you left. They welcomed me with open arms, then died within a few months of each other shortly after our reunion. Amazingly, they left the house to me. Pretty special, huh?'

It had been a beautiful gesture and she liked to think they'd come to love her as much as she'd loved them in the short time they'd had together.

'Sure is. I'm glad you had someone to look out for you.'

He dropped his hand and insanely she missed his warm touch.

This wasn't good. Curiosity was one thing, kissing him and opening up to him about her grandparents was in another realm. She needed to get home before she really lost it and told him a few other deep, dark secrets.

'Look, I really have to go,' she said, her voice harsh and cold considering they'd just been making small talk.

'What's wrong?'

He stared at her and raised an eyebrow as if he couldn't fathom what he was looking at and she hated the traitorous leap of her heart that the hint of concern in his voice might actually mean he cared.

'Nothing, why?'

'You're wound tighter than a spring. You used to be spontaneous and eager and able to laugh at yourself. What happened? Did inheriting the family jewels change you?'

She clenched her fists, barely registering the sting of fingernails biting into her palms when all she felt like doing was kneeing him in *his* family jewels.

'I'm just tired. Besides, you don't know the first thing about me any more.'

He straightened and she had to tilt her head to look up at him. 'That's where you're wrong. We used to have a connection and I intend to use the week ahead to catch up.'

Catch up.

Two simple words that held a staggering array of connotations, of the various ways in which they could catch up, and her heart flipped in a perfect somersault with double pike at the thought.

Sighing, she followed him to the doorway and, before they walked through it, reached out and touched his arm.

'Why are you doing this, Ty?'

He stopped and swivelled to face her, his features softening. 'You haven't called me that in a long time.'

'It's been a long time,' she responded, suddenly saddened by their lack of contact over the years. 'Now answer my question.'

He shrugged. 'A week isn't all that long and I'm a sucker for a good cause. The orphanage is home to those poor little kids and they deserve a chance in life.'

She'd meant why was he doing this to them, insisting they spend a week together when they'd been finished for years.

However, she let it slide for now, the sadness creeping across his face telling her how much he sympathised with the orphans.

'Still the same old Ty? Always out to save the world.'

'It's what I do. Why do you make it sound like I'm on an ego trip or something?'

'Aren't you?'

He swore softly and she changed tack. 'Are you on leave?'

'Yeah, one week.'

'Why didn't you just donate money rather than giving up your week?'

The thought had niggled since she'd seen his name on the list of prospective guys for sale. His job had always come first and she doubted that would have changed. After all, it was one of the things that had driven them apart.

He shrugged and looked away. 'I thought the auction might raise more money than I could give.'

He was lying.

She knew it the minute he glanced away. Ty was as straight as they came. He always looked a person in the eye and called a spade a shovel, which made his reticence to discuss this all the more intriguing. He'd been a stand-up guy when they'd first met, too much so if his blunt declaration their marriage would never work with one absentee partner all the time had been any indication.

'There's more to this. You're hiding something.'

'Still the snoop, eh? You won't find your next story here.'

This time he looked straight at her, something akin to challenge etched in the darkening depths of his eyes.

If there was one thing she thrived on it was a challenge and sailor boy knew it.

'Maybe not, but you can't blame a girl for trying. Perhaps I should just let it all go and agree to this crazy scheme, and then use it to my full advantage.'

Not that she'd seriously contemplate spending the week

with him, but it was nice to gain the upper hand with Mr Confidence.

His voice dropped, low and husky, eliciting a whole host of visceral reactions she'd rather not decipher.

'Now you're talking. If you let it all go this week could be more fun than I thought.'

He ran his hands lightly over her upper arms in a soft caress and her legs trembled, her desire needing little to rekindle. One touch. That was all it took to make her burn for him just as she used to.

So much for gaining the upper hand.

'Goodnight, Ty.'

She spun on her heel and strode away, eager to put as much distance between them as possible.

His taunting laughter followed her down the long corridor. 'You can run but you can't hide.'

'Wanna make a bet?' she mumbled as she lengthened her stride and hoped to God that Di had waited for her.

CHAPTER THREE

'AREN'T you the dark horse? Fancy waiting to the end to bid and snaffling the best of the lot.'

Kate had been grateful Di had waited for her after the auction. And, clearly realising her boss needed some space on the trip back to the office, Di hadn't asked her any questions. Apparently now, though, she was fair game.

'Don't you have work to do?' Kate shuffled papers around, hoping to get rid of Di pronto.

Predictably, it didn't work. The woman had an inquisitive nature worthy of an up-and-comer in the publishing business.

Di perched on the edge of her desk and shoved aside the papers Kate had been fiddling with. 'Nothing that can't wait. Come on, spill the beans. Where did you two disappear to after the show? In a cosy little friendship bracelet, no less.'

Kate sighed, pushing the thought of Ty's dynamic kiss to the far recesses of her mind.

'There's nothing to tell. We unlocked ourselves, had a chat to establish boundaries and that was it.'

Di pounced on her. 'Aha! I knew it. Why would you need to establish boundaries? Did something happen between the dishy SEAL and my intrepid boss?'

'Ex-SEAL,' she corrected automatically.

'How do you know that?'

Great, she thought. Slip up number two in less than a minute. Di was no slouch, which was why she'd hired her.

She could've fluffed her way out of it and rambled on about the announcer saying he was an instructor these days, but she knew Di wouldn't let up until she had nothing less than the truth.

'I know Tyler James.'

A deafening silence followed her revelation till Di let out a squeal. 'Ooh, I knew there was more to you than meets the eye. Here I am feeling sorry for my workaholic old boss and she's out there running around with hot sailors.'

'Hey! Enough of the old stuff and I'm not running around with anybody. I met Tyler about six years ago when he was a SEAL. He isn't just an instructor. He's had his fair share of action.'

Both in and out of uniform and lucky for her she'd been privy to Ty at his best.

'I just bet he has,' purred the younger woman.

'For heaven's sake, get your mind out of the gutter.'

'Why, when it's so much fun?'

Di slid off the desk and wandered around the office, trying to look nonchalant and failing miserably. 'Is that why you put in a bid, boss? Looking for a little action?'

Kate threw a pencil at her. 'Out. Now. Get back to work before you're fired.'

'You wouldn't dare. I'm your right-hand gal.'

Di smirked and flounced out of the room, her bright orange skirt swishing around her ankles.

Kate sat back and laughed. Di was right. She was the best PA she'd ever had and, what was worse, the young woman knew it. However, why did she have to be so accurate in her assumptions about Kate's nonexistent love life?

Seeing Ty had awakened her dormant hormones in a big way; her skin still tingled at the memory of his hands rubbing her wrist. No man had ever affected her as he did.

He'd been a dynamite lover, her first, but despite that mind-blowing kiss earlier she had no intention of revisiting that part of her life.

Though in all honesty if she hadn't been bound at the time there was no telling what her hands would've been tempted to do and she squirmed in her seat at the recollection. For a twenty-seven-year-old at the top of her game, her little 'let's get reacquainted' experience with Ty had hot-wired her libido and how.

The phone ringing brought her back to the present.

'Kate Hayden speaking.'

'So, you did go back to the office. I thought that was just an excuse to escape.'

Ty's husky tone did little to calm her racing pulse. If anything, the sound of his deep voice fuelled the fantasy she'd just been indulging in. Stupid, stupid, stupid.

'You think I was trying to escape?'

His low chuckle fired her nerve-endings. 'Oh, call it a feeling. You weren't exactly falling all over me earlier this evening.'

She kept her voice deliberately cool, trying to ignore the erotic memory of their entwined bodies reflected in the mirror that leaped to mind. If that wasn't falling all over him she didn't know what was.

'It isn't every day a girl acquires an Odd Bod. Perhaps I was just nervous?'

She doodled on the pad in front of her, almost falling off her chair when she realised she was drawing large hearts with the initials K.H. and T.J. intertwined.

'Yeah, right. The Kate I know is never nervous. Confident and bossy maybe. Nervous? No way.'

'You forgot gorgeous,' she murmured, wondering where the breathy voice came from.

She shouldn't flirt with him, she really shouldn't, but somehow he brought out that side of her without trying and she heard a sharp intake of breath on the other end of the line.

'That goes without saying.' He paused for a moment. 'Are you flirting with me, sweetheart?'

The endearment thrilled her, though she knew it was a game with him and suddenly, just like the old days, she joined in with gusto.

'What if I am? I'm a woman, you're an Odd Bod. Why not?'

'Lady, you're a chameleon. One minute you can't get away from me quick enough, the next you're sounding like Mae West. Why don't I come up and see you some time?'

She leaned back in her leather chair, crossed her ankles and stared out at the twinkling lights of downtown LA, spread out like a fairyland forty storeys below. She adored this view, loved the hip city vibe, yet somehow sitting here chatting to Ty inspired her more than the vista she admired on a daily basis.

Playing with him was fun, even if she had no intention of following through, and it had been so long since she'd had any fun. How far could she push him?

'What are you doing right now?'

Once again, silence greeted her.

'Ty, still there?'

'Yeah. Where did you say your office was?'

His voice dropped lower, reminding her of the intimacy they'd shared all those years ago when she'd hung on his every word.

'I didn't. Though if I let it all go like I mentioned earlier, I could invite you for a coffee at my place…'

Yeah, like that was going to happen. There was only so much her hormones could take and teasing him like this, flirting with him, was bad enough.

'Do you mean coffee…or *coffee*?'

A delicious tingle ran up her spine and she knew for a fact he would give her a better buzz than any caffeine fix: rich, warm, addictive. And the high would last a heck of a lot longer.

'Boss, I'm leaving.' Di's voice startled her as she stuck her head around the door.

Kate sat up straight. 'Can you hold on a sec?' she said into the receiver and covered it with her hand.

'Sure thing, Katie,' he murmured, sending heat flooding into her cheeks.

'Who's that?' mouthed Di.

'Nobody important. You head off.'

'Whatever you say, boss.' With a wink and a blown kiss, Di left the office.

Kate took a steadying breath, almost relieved at the reprieve, and removed her hand from the phone. 'Sorry about that.'

'So, I'm nobody, huh? Nice.'

She smiled at the thought of bruising Ty's ego. 'I didn't mean it like that.'

'What did you mean, then? If I'm not nobody I must be somebody?'

His probing question sent doubt spiralling through her. What was she doing encouraging him when she'd already made up her mind to ditch him first thing tomorrow morning when she'd had time to gather her wits?

Damn it, he'd always had the power to do this, to tie her up in knots till she couldn't think straight.

'Look, I'm tired. It's been a long night and I've got one more article to edit before I leave. We'll catch up tomorrow, okay?'

His silence did little to soothe her frazzled nerves.

'Ty?'

'You're running scared.'

She swallowed, trying to ease the sudden dryness in her throat. 'I don't know what you're talking about.'

He chuckled, deep and low, the familiar sound skittering across her skin, raising tiny goose-bumps.

'Yeah, you do. Shame. I thought you might want to pick up where we left off.'

'You wish.'

The image of their parting six years ago flashed into her

mind. It had been touch and go; he'd touched her all over her body, initiating her into pleasures she'd only dreamed about before pulling away from her by running back to his precious job, and she'd gone the same way, burying herself in a new job as far away from him as she could get.

Now he was back. Just as gorgeous, just as charming and just as dangerous to her peace of mind as ever if she was foolish enough to let him in.

'Oh, yeah, I wish.' He paused, as if choosing his words carefully. 'By the way, why are you working after eleven?'

'The usual. Deadlines to meet. Nothing out of the ordinary.' She sounded weary, even to her ears.

'Don't you have a life?'

Her brittle laugh echoed around the empty office. 'This is my life.'

She didn't add that it was about all she had.

'You really need to get out more. I'm going to make it my personal goal to ensure you live a little over the next week. Deal?'

'It's not going to happen.'

Her brisk reply sounded strained and, though the thought of Ty helping her to 'live a little' conjured up some wild images, she'd done enough fantasising for one evening and had to put an end to this ASAP.

He ignored her rebuttal, his low chuckles sounding way too confident.

'I'll call you tomorrow. Pleasant dreams, Katie.'

As the dial tone hummed she knew that dreams would be impossible tonight. She needed to sleep in order to dream and she seriously doubted that she could nod off after the evening she'd just had.

Tyler James was her history.

Then why did he feel startlingly like the present?

* * *

Tyler was too wound up to sleep. Shrugging into a bomber jacket, he picked up his keys and headed out the door.

Living near the base had its advantages. Dropping into the rec hall for a drink meant he was bound to run into someone he knew and, though usually reticent, he felt like company tonight. Perhaps trading a few jokes with the boys might take the edge off?

He doubted it. Only one thing could take the edge off and she was buried in some uptown office, her nose to the grindstone.

Kate's hot little act on the phone had pushed all his buttons. If only her assistant hadn't interrupted he could be holed up in her house right now sharing more than coffee.

And, boy, did he need it.

Seeing her again had him remembering all too well the contours of her curves beneath his hands, the eager sounds she made during sex, the way she made him feel as if he were the only man in the world for her.

Unfortunately, that couldn't be true. He wasn't a total idiot and a vibrant woman like her would have had a string of guys panting after her since they'd parted.

He clenched his hands into fists, hating the irrational surge of jealousy stabbing through him. He'd moved on and hadn't exactly lived like a monk himself in the last six years so what did he expect—for a stunner like Kate to sit around twiddling her thumbs?

Gritting his teeth, he picked up the pace and entered the rec hall. He didn't need this complicating his life. Never had.

What Kate did with her life and who she spent it with had nothing to do with him. He valued his independence and answering to number one suited him just fine and, despite the unexpected pleasure of having Kate reappear at this point in his life, he had no intention of getting sucked back into the confusing whirlpool their relationship had become towards the end.

Instead, he'd consider this chance encounter as a surprise

gift dropped in his lap, one he had every intention of unwrapping and enjoying at his leisure over the next week before he had his annual physical and potentially had his career ripped out from under him.

'Hey, TJ. What's happening?'

He looked up, more than glad to see the big guy in front of him, and stuck out his hand. 'Hey, Bear. What're you doing here? Thought Team Eight was on leave at the moment?'

'Nah, got called back last night. So much for a little R and R.'

Tyler laughed. 'The Chief pushing you too hard these days, huh? Want a beer?'

Bear nodded and pulled out a chair, turning it backwards before sitting. He'd never seen his giant friend sit any other way.

'Yeah, the Chief is always pushing for more. You know the drill.'

Tyler nodded and placed the drinks on the table. 'Yeah, I do. Cheers.'

They clinked bottles and lapsed into silence. As Tyler took a long swig of icy cold beer he thanked the Lord that Evan 'Bear' Bridges had chosen tonight to walk into the rec hall. He could do with a friend.

'What's up? You look like hell, man.'

Tyler set his bottle down. 'That obvious?'

'Uh-huh. Tell old Bear all about it.'

He leaned back and crossed his arms. 'It's the orphanage. Looks like it's going to shut down.'

Bear's eyes widened. 'No way. With the amount of cash you donate out of your wages each year the joint should be open into the next century.'

''Fraid not. Looks like the place is in trouble.'

'Anything I can do?' His friend reached towards his back pocket as if ready to pull out his wallet.

'Not unless you can rustle up a quick half-million dollars.'

Bear shook his head. 'No can do, bro. Sorry.'

'I'm the one who's sorry,' he muttered, feeling helpless for only the third time in his life and not relishing the emotion one bit. The first time had been when he'd walked out on Kate, the second when he'd blown his knee, and he felt just as useless now.

SEALs were renowned for their innovation, their ingenuity, their persistence. So why the hell couldn't he do more for the one cause that meant everything to him?

At that moment, their chief, Jack Crawford, strolled into the bar and headed straight towards them.

'Howdy, Bear. Thought you were on leave, TJ?'

Tyler grabbed the proffered hand and shook it. 'I am.'

'Then what are you doing here?'

Tyler downed the rest of his beer. 'Business.'

'I bet.'

He couldn't fathom the reason behind Jack's sly grin.

'Been to any auctions lately?'

Though the question seemed innocuous enough, combined with Jack's smirk, Tyler knew his secret was out.

'Ha, ha. How did you find out?'

Bear's head turned from side to side as if watching a tennis match. 'What are you clowns talking about?'

Jack's grin widened. 'Didn't you hear the news? TJ's latest mission involves being shackled to a woman for a week doing all her *odd jobs*.'

Bear guffawed loudly. 'You're kidding me, right? Why the hell would you do a fool thing like that?'

'For charity, of course.'

Tyler glared meaningfully at Bear, hoping he'd get the drift. His friend was the only one who knew about his upbringing at the orphanage and he wanted to keep it that way. He'd had enough pity to last him a lifetime growing up, he sure as hell didn't need any from his colleagues now.

Bear cottoned on quickly. He merely quirked an eyebrow and chugged on his beer.

Thankfully, Jack relented. 'Yeah, I agree that the orphanage is a good cause. Though I reckon there's more behind this, TJ. I reckon you like being at the beck and call of some fancy dame.'

'Who told you she's fancy?' Tyler chuckled, envisaging how Kate would respond to being described as 'fancy'.

'Leila was at the auction. She just got home, bursting with the news about you and that magazine editor. Said that sparks were flying and that was before the shackles went on.'

Tyler's gut tightened. The image of being bound to Kate did it. At least thinking about the orphanage had distracted him from her memory. For a good ten minutes, anyway.

He leaned back, trying to instil a measure of casualness into his voice. 'I think Leila has a great imagination. There were no sparks. I'm just donating my time for a good cause.'

'Yeah, right. So what if this editor looks like a supermodel? All part of the job, huh?' Jack's cheesy grin grew wider by the second.

'Damn sure.' Tyler pushed back his chair. 'Sorry, guys. Much as I'd like to hang around, I have to go. Early start. O-six hundred.'

Suddenly, his need for company had vanished. He'd come here to erase Kate from his memory bank, not discuss her, and he knew the boys. Once they got started they would want to hear every last detail. He waved and walked away, leaving his two closest friends grinning in his wake.

'See you in a week, TJ. If you survive, that is.'

Ignoring Jack's final taunt, he headed out into the balmy Californian night. There was no doubt in his mind that he would survive. After all, he'd handled tougher missions and come out unscathed.

Once again, a vision of Kate's gold-flecked hazel eyes

flashed into his mind, closely followed by the memory of their searing kiss.

He just hoped this mission wasn't about to become his nemesis.

Kate prided herself on being cool, organised and professional at all times. To do this she needed at least eight solid hours of sleep a night. Without it she turned into a monster, as all her staff knew. Unfortunately, last night hadn't been conducive to sleeping and she was paying the price now. So would anyone else who crossed her path today.

'Good morning, boss. Sleep well?' Di strolled into her office, all blonde spikes and cheerfulness.

'Is it? And no. Where's that damn article on homeless shelters?'

She shuffled around her desk, sending papers flying in all directions while making a frantic grab for her take-out skinny latte.

What happened to organised and professional? Right now her desk resembled a second-grader's with the writing strewn across it probably making about that much sense.

'Didn't sleep too well? Can't blame you.'

Kate didn't like the twinkle in her assistant's eye. Besides, how could Di be so darn chirpy every morning? Didn't she ever wake up with a sore head?

'What's that supposed to mean?'

Kate finally stopped rummaging around and sat back, draining the last of her coffee, lobbing the cup in the bin and rubbing her temples. She rarely drank and the three glasses of champagne last night combined with the haunting image of Ty looking better than ever had kept her tossing and turning all night.

'Oh, nothing.' Di's grin broadened. 'Though if I had the prospect of some sexy sailor trailing after me all week I wouldn't be able to get any shut-eye either.'

'He's not trailing after me,' she snapped, her headache intensifying by the minute.

'Oh, yes, he is. He's just stepped out of the lift and is heading this way.'

Kate sat bolt upright in time to see Ty honing in on her office. Great. Just great.

Di wiggled her fingers in a saucy wave and strolled away, giving Tyler a similar wave, and Kate tried to ignore the absurd jolt of jealousy that shot through her. Ty was her past and she shouldn't have to remind herself of that fact.

He walked straight into her office as if he owned the place. 'Hi. Got a minute?'

How dared he look so good at this hour of the morning? Faded denim jeans hugged his long legs and a white T-shirt moulded his muscular torso like a second skin, delineating every single layer of taut, hard muscle beneath it. The type of muscle she used to love running her hands over, caressing, skimming, relishing.

Okay, maybe good was an understatement. Try delectable and she struggled not to drool.

'What are you doing here?'

Though she tried to keep her voice cool, it came out all high and squeaky.

A smile tugged at the corners of his delicious mouth. 'Still not a morning person, huh?'

She shook her head and wished she hadn't as the pounding in her brain increased.

'I'm surprised you remember.'

'How could I forget?'

He flashed his trademark killer smile, the one that always made her knees go weak. Thankfully, she was sitting down.

'So, what else do you remember?'

He closed the door and strode across the room in one lithe

movement. She loved how he walked. Correction, how he stalked, all stealth and fluid lines, and her pulse accelerated in anticipation as he perched on the corner of her desk less than two feet away.

'I remember plenty.'

He tipped up her chin, stroking her cheek with his thumb in the barest of touches as she stared, trapped beneath his scrutinising gaze, his thumb doing crazy things to her insides as it grazed her skin slowly, repeatedly.

'Yeah, well, I do too.'

She leaned back, breaking the tenuous contact that was wreaking havoc with her senses. 'But that's all they are, just memories.'

His eyes narrowed to slivers of electrifying blue. 'Yeah, but they were good. Damn good. And you know it.'

She glared, the jackhammering in her head intensifying as she tried to put words together in a coherent fashion , her brain befuddled by his closeness, his touch.

'All I know is I've got a lot of work to do and sitting here talking about ancient history is wasting my time.'

Thankfully, his thumb had stopped stroking her cheek. On the downside, he re-established contact by trailing his index finger along her jaw-line, setting her nerve-endings alight.

'What's with the attitude? You said we'd talk in the morning. Aren't you glad to see me?'

She pulled away from his blazing touch. 'We'll talk later. I haven't got time for this now.'

He grinned, sending her pulse rate into overdrive. 'You didn't answer my question.'

'About the memories, the attitude or being happy to see you?'

There was no way she would answer any of his questions. She'd made a fool of herself last night. Questions only led to answers and they led directly to trouble.

'How about all of the above?'

'Look, I'd love to chat but I've got important deadlines to meet.'

She tried to stare him down. It had been a game with them, a battle of wills to see who would look away first. She'd always lost but not today.

He sat back and folded his arms, looking way too cocky, the corners of his mouth curving into a tempting smile.

'Surely Lois Lane can take a break for a few minutes?'

'Nope, sorry, no can do. I'm busy.'

She picked up a few papers and rattled them for good measure, needing to look away from his intense stare and that sexy smile. He still had the power to reduce her to a blathering mess with just one look—not that she'd let him know that.

'Aren't you the least bit curious?'

'About?'

'Why I'm here. Where I've been. What I've been doing. You must be otherwise you wouldn't have paid a small fortune to have me last night.'

Sighing, she pushed away from the desk, grateful to establish some distance between them. 'You're never going to let me forget that, are you?'

His smile couldn't get any smugger if he tried. 'Not on your life.'

Her heart clenched at the seductive glint in his eyes, the same twinkle that had prompted her to do all sorts of crazy things six years earlier.

He'd always had this power over her, teasing her, infuriating her, making her fall in love when it was the last thing she'd expected.

Unfortunately, it looked as if he still held that same power to make her contemplate all sorts of nutty things, like make her bid for him when the last thing she wanted was to have him trailing after her for a week.

'Okay, you win. Let's get this sorted now so I can get back

to work. You really can't be serious about wanting to go through with this odd-jobs stuff?'

He leaned forward, the depth of his blue eyes leaving her breathless as his voice dropped an octave lower. 'Why not? It'll be fun.'

She didn't have time for fun. Maybe the girls were right, she was stuck in her ways and a workaholic: uptight, frustrated and alone.

Logically, she should never have attended the auction if she hadn't wanted a confrontation with Ty and now that she'd had it, he'd kissed her silly and resurrected memories better left forgotten, she needed to get rid of him once and for all.

'That may well be,' she said, aiming for cool and botching it horribly when heat surged into her cheeks at his triumphant expression, 'but I don't think it's a good idea.'

'I do.'

He slid off her desk and sauntered towards the door, leaving her with a great view of the sexy butt she'd grabbed on numerous lucky occasions, turning to face her before he left. 'It's going to be great catching up. Just like old times.'

Kate stiffened.

Just like old times.

Images of fun-filled days at the beach and long, hot, sultry Californian nights spent making love on top of twisted sheets sprang to mind and she wondered if time had enhanced her memories or if it really had been that good between her and Ty.

'Katie?'

'My answer is no, Ty.'

She blinked several times, hoping he couldn't read her thoughts as he used to.

'I still want you too.'

With that he sauntered out the door, leaving her open-mouthed before she snapped her jaw shut, wishing she'd had the final word.

The guy was infuriating.

The guy was cocky.

The guy was right.

She did want him, with every cell in her oversensitised body, and the feeling was mutual?

Oh, boy.

'You're crazy,' she muttered, sinking into her chair and picking up the overworked stress ball on her desk and squeezing as if her life depended on it. It didn't help. The rubber ball looked a bit like her, worn out, frayed around the edges, with all the life crushed out of it.

She threw the ball into the bin and leaped to her feet. If she rushed after Ty she just might make it. He hadn't accepted her refusal and she needed to ram home her point that the last thing she wanted to do was spend the next week with him.

However, as she yanked open the door she ran straight into her boss.

'Whoa. Where's the fire?'

Henry Kerr, *Femme*'s Chief Editor, settled her back on her feet. He always managed to catch her at a bad time. In fact, she was convinced he had radar for trouble and it was tuned in to her frequency.

'Sorry. In a hurry.'

He quirked an eyebrow. 'So I see. Got a minute?'

She knew by the serious look on his face that it wasn't a question, it was an order. So much for chasing after Ty.

'Sure. What's up?'

He smiled and she knew she was in trouble. Her boss never smiled unless she'd done something wrong. 'Come into my office and I'll let you in on a secret.'

She followed him, slouching along in the same way she usually followed the dentist into his rooms, though she hoped her meeting with Henry didn't involve anything as difficult or painful as pulling teeth. The memory of her first and last tooth removed as a nine-year-old still rankled.

Henry closed the door and gestured towards a chair. 'Have a seat and we'll get down to business.'

Here it comes, the injection and the drill.

Henry sat down behind his desk and rested his folded hands on his paunch. 'Good work last night, Kate. Real good.'

Huh?

She smiled and nodded, not having the faintest idea what he was talking about.

'Buying that Navy guy was a stroke of genius on your part. Unbelievable. Pure gold.'

Okay, now she knew something was up. Her boss was impressed with the stupidest thing she'd done in a long time?

Thankfully, she didn't have to reply as Henry continued, 'The publicity in the papers today is worth a mint on its own, but have you seen the pictures we've got? Amazing. Just what the magazine needs. A real-life story about one of its own. Good one, Kate.'

She didn't like the sound of this. Clasping her hands in her lap, she counted to ten, slowly. 'I'm an editor, not a news story.'

He chuckled, a deep belly laugh that caused his three chins to wobble in succession. 'That's where you're wrong. Our phones haven't stopped ringing all morning. All the reporters want to talk to our newest star and I've told them to back off. They can read all about it in the upcoming issue of *Femme*. Like I said, pure gold.'

She rarely argued with her boss but decided that today was a day for firsts.

'This isn't a good idea. I don't want my credibility to suffer. I've worked long and hard to get where I am. You know that.'

Thankfully, Henry had stopped chuckling but his sly

grin worried her even more. 'Don't worry about your credibility. What could be more credible than being appointed Chief Editor?'

'Pardon?'

She could have sworn that he'd just uttered the words she'd wanted to hear for ever.

'You heard me. The job's yours if you want it.'

He beamed like Santa Claus and for a minute she believed that all her Christmases had come at once. Until reality set in.

'You know how much I'd love your job, Henry. But that's just it. It's *your* job.'

'Not any more. I'm retiring in the next few months and I want you to be the next chief. How about it?'

It wasn't a joke. Though Henry was smiling she knew he wouldn't make her an offer like this unless he was genuine.

'If you're serious, I'll take it.'

She finally allowed her face muscles to relax into what she hoped was a smile. She hadn't realised till that moment just how tense she'd been.

'Good. That's settled.' He leaned back in his chair looking like the proverbial cat that had swallowed the canary. 'Just one more thing.'

'Yes?'

'The magazine has to run that feature story on the auction last night and your acquisition.'

'Are you bribing me? The promotion for the story?'

Kate didn't like bribes. Never had. Not since the early days when her father had tried to buy her love with meaningless trinkets on his all-too-brief visits home.

Henry smiled and rested his steepled fingers on his chest. 'Got it in one. So, is it a deal?'

This was an opportunity of a lifetime. She'd coveted Henry's job for as long as she could remember and here it was being offered to her on a plate. And all she had to do was one story? Why was she hesitating?

Ty.

She didn't want to spend a week with him and had just told him so.

What would he think if she back-pedalled? Would he take it as a sign she did still want him?

Why did this have to be so complicated? She'd wanted this promotion for ever. Why did getting it have to involve Ty? Could she put up with him for a week—and all the possible ramifications—for the job of a lifetime?

Deep down, she knew the decision was a no-brainer. She was a journo at heart, a career girl with places to go, and nothing would stand in her way. Nothing.

'You've got yourself a new chief.'

She shook Henry's hand, crossing her fingers behind her back, for luck with the other.

Ty would come to the party. He had to.

Though did she really want him to?

Doing this story meant spending time with him and possibly more, so much more.

And she had no idea if she was ready for it.

CHAPTER FOUR

TYLER stabbed at the buttons of the elevator, wishing the damn thing would move faster. He hated skyscrapers. Give him rescue operations any day. Buildings stifled him, made him feel bulky and out of place and he'd had a lifetime of feeling like that, of not belonging.

However, his building phobia faded as he stepped into the elevator. Instead, a sexy vision of Kate perched behind her cushy desk, her hair slicked back in some weird bun arrangement and her hot body sheathed in a tight-fitting fire-engine-red suit had imprinted itself on his brain and he couldn't budge it.

She had him squirming, no two ways about it. He couldn't get her out of his head and though he hadn't got a handle on why she'd 'bought' him in the first place only to renege on the week ahead, he didn't care.

Why waste time trying to analyse the female psyche? He'd be better off interrogating terrorists for Intel; at least he'd have more chance of getting answers.

No, he wouldn't question this unexpected gift. For that was exactly what spending a week with his sultry ex would be, especially considering he could be a washed-up ex-SEAL this time next week.

And she would spend the week with him, despite her protests to the contrary. He'd make sure of it.

He might have been out of the action for a while now but his persuasive powers weren't that rusty. And if he could convince his current charges to crash through a burning wall if needed, he was pretty damn sure he could change Kate's mind.

As the elevator doors opened his mobile phone vibrated against his hip.

'TJ here.'

He strode across the foyer, eager to get outside and feel the warm Californian sunshine on his face before he was tempted to head back up to Kate's office and convince her that her fancy-schmancy desk could be used for a lot more fun activities than work.

'Ty?'

Her almost-whisper slammed into his conscious. Damn, why did she have to say his name like that, all soft and breathy as if she'd just woken up? His libido, already fully revved up by the sight of her a few minutes ago, went into overdrive at the sound of her sexy voice.

'Miss me already, huh?'

She paused and he wished for one, irrational moment that she'd say 'you bet'.

Dream on, lover boy. There was about as much chance of that happening as he had of returning to active duty. His knee was blown just like any chance he had of more than a casual, fun week with his luscious ex.

'Uh…I was wondering if you were free for lunch.'

He heard the uncertainty in her voice and wondered what had happened to the feisty, confident 'get out of my life' Kate. He'd been intrigued by her motivation to buy him, still was. Now, after practically shoving him out the door she was asking to see him in a few hours?

Shaking his head, he grinned. He'd never figure her out.

'What did you have in mind?'

She sighed, a small sound that shot straight to his groin. Damn, he had it bad.

'How about meeting at Venice Beach?'

Ty gripped the phone, wondering if she remembered the first time he'd taken her there and how that day had ended in an unexpected explosion of passion when she'd clung to him, soft and needy in the back seat of his SUV, and he'd lost his mind. She'd made him squirm back then and it looked as if nothing had changed.

'Fine. What time?'

'Midday? At Whippy's?'

Yeah, she remembered all right.

'Sounds like a plan.'

Now, if he could keep his cool and not jump her as his instincts had been urging him to since he'd seen her last night he'd be doing great.

'See you then.'

She hung up on him and he snapped his phone shut, confused as hell but looking forward to seeing the cause of his angst much sooner than he'd anticipated.

Kate loved the Venice Beach vibe. Jugglers and buskers vied for attention alongside muscle men and in-line skaters clad in teensy-weensy bikinis, with an eclectic blend of tourists and food vendors thrown in for good measure.

The place was buzzing any time of day or night and she often headed here in her limited down time to soak up the atmosphere and indulge in her favourite pastime, people-watching. It stirred her like no other part of LA, a bit like the guy who had introduced her to this part of town.

As if on cue Ty sauntered towards her, his long strides eating up the boardwalk, and all she could do was stare, feasting her eyes on the striking vision he made in hip-hugging jeans and white cotton T.

'Hi.'

She pasted a smile on her face, willing her heart to stop pounding so she'd have a chance of hearing his reply.

'Hey. You changed.'

His gaze slid up her body, lingered on her breasts for an appreciative second before fixing on her mouth.

And you noticed.

She shrugged, her skin burning from the intensity of his gaze. 'Yeah, well, the corporate look doesn't quite fit in down here.'

He laughed and the rich, deep sound washed over her, warming her better than the sun's rays. 'You can say that again. Besides, I prefer what you're wearing now.'

Kate gulped, trying to ease the tension of her constricted throat muscles. The cargoes, pink T-shirt and sneakers were the only casual items she carried in her gym bag for changing into after a workout. Not exactly seduction material.

But then, who said anything about seduction?

'Want an ice cream?' she blurted, anxious to break the tension that enveloped them, the same tension that caused her to do crazy things like bid on him at a public auction, the same tension that had always zinged between them and amazingly hadn't waned.

If anything, the sparks they generated now were fiercer than six years ago and she knew without a doubt they'd ignite into a blazing conflagration given a little oxygen.

'Yeah, I could do with something to cool me down.'

Great. Was he saying he was hot for her or was it a throwaway comment on the LA weather?

'Same as usual?'

She nodded, wondering how he remembered a small, insignificant fact like her favourite ice-cream flavour and thrilled that he did.

After ordering and paying he handed her a choc-mint

waffle cone and their fingers brushed. An electrifying charge raced up her arm and she would have dropped the ice cream if he hadn't pulled away faster than she could blink.

So much for wanting to touch her. He must have been talking about the weather after all.

'Mmm…' She licked the sticky glob of ice cream, savouring the icy tingle as it slid down her throat.

A strange choking sound came from Ty's direction and she looked up to find his gaze fixed on her mouth.

Letting her know she'd been wrong. It wasn't the sun that had raised his temperature to the point he needed cooling down; given it was his fault she was in this current awful situation perhaps it was time for a little payback.

'Isn't this the best?' she murmured, taking a long, leisurely swipe at the rim of the cone with her tongue.

Desire, swift and fierce, blazed in his eyes as his gaze stayed riveted to her tongue. She licked the rivulets running down the side of the cone before running her tongue along her upper lip, every flick a slow, torturous attempt at teasing him.

He gripped his ice-cream cone, it snapped and as if in slow motion the scoop fell and landed on the pavement, quickly forming a molten mess of rum'n'raisin.

'Oh,' she said, trying to hide her grin behind her cone.

'Too bad. Now I'll have to share yours.'

In an instant he'd wrapped his hand around hers and brought her ice cream to his mouth and it was her turn to squirm as he licked her ice cream in what could only be described as an extremely indecent way to eat a dessert in public.

Watching his tongue, she had a sudden wish to be every flavour under the sun, though the way her body burned she'd be lying in a puddle like the scoop on the hot concrete.

'Not bad,' he drawled, pulling back a fraction but not letting go of her hand.

Kate didn't know how long they stood that way, gazes

locked, hands clenched around the cone. It seemed like an eternity and in a sudden flash of clarity, she knew.

This man was going to rock her world all over again.

He let go of her hand and stepped away, leaving her feeling slightly chilled despite the midday sun.

'So I'm guessing you didn't just want to meet down here for the ice cream?'

She nodded. 'I was hoping we could talk.'

'About?'

'The week ahead. And a woman's prerogative to change her mind.'

'This sounds interesting.' He sat on a nearby bench and patted the space next to him. 'Guess I was right.'

'About?'

She scowled at him; he didn't have to spell it out. The minute his heated gaze locked on hers, she knew he was referring to his parting comment about her still wanting him as much as he wanted her.

Grinning, he said, 'You know you're making too much of this, right? It's no big deal. We get to catch up, maybe have a laugh over old times. Like I said, no biggie.'

She ditched the remainder of her ice cream in the bin and sat beside him, her gut churning. No biggie? Who was he kidding? Spending a week with the sexiest guy on the planet was a big deal no matter how much he tried to play it down.

'Okay, so I change my mind and we get to play catch-up. I was also wondering if you'd do me a favour.'

He leaned back and rested his arm across the back of the bench, the light dusting of dark hair along his muscular forearm grabbing her attention. Most of her friends had a thing for guy's butts. Personally, she had a thing for forearms. The more muscly, the better, and Ty had two of the best.

'Depends on what it is.'

His teasing smile lit up his face and she wondered how long that would last once he heard what she had to say.

She took a steadying breath. 'Being my odd-job guy is going to involve more than you might be prepared for.'

'I think I can handle anything you dish out.'

The lines around his eyes crinkled adorably and it took every inch of will-power not to reach out and smooth them.

She'd always loved this teasing side of him and they'd often bounced off each other, trading quips with incredible speed.

A huge part of her wanted to pick up where they'd left off and swap one-liners like a pro but she couldn't. She wouldn't let her guard down around him completely. She couldn't.

Funny things might happen if she did that, like her falling for him a second time around, and, for a savvy career woman who knew what she wanted these days and went out and got it, that would be very, very stupid.

'I'm not a mind-reader, Katie, so spit it out. It can't be that bad, right?'

As if making it easier on her he looked away and she drank in the sight of the sun skimming his tanned face, etching the hard planes and angles in shades of bronze, and in an instant she was transported back to the first time they'd come here.

Strolling along the boardwalk hand in hand at dusk, sharing fish and chips on the beach before snuggling in the back of his SUV.

Heat surged into her cheeks at the recollection of how far that snuggling had gone, how incredible Ty had made her feel.

'Katie?'

He sat up suddenly and fixed her with a piercing stare that drove all rational thought from her mind as she struggled not to re-enact the erotic images flashing through her mind a second before, wishing she could pick up the conversation thread but coming up a total blank.

Something about the week ahead… The words starting to form turned to dust as their gazes locked, heated and combusted and before she knew how it had happened his hand skimmed her neck and she leaned towards him, powerless to resist the irrational urge to taste him once again.

'This is crazy,' he muttered against the side of her mouth as their lips melded in a blaze of heat, intense, burning, erotic.

She clutched at his chest as if she were drowning, sliding her hands along the hard contours before dropping lower, the familiar ridges of his six-pack tantalising her exploring fingertips through the cotton of his T-shirt, and she itched to touch his bare skin, to feel the smooth, silky hardness she'd known in the past.

Angling her head slightly, she gave him access to her craving mouth, wanting more, wanting all of him. His teeth nibbled her lower lip before his tongue eased into her mouth, tasting and stroking every inch of the way. He tasted delicious, the intoxicating combination of choc-mint and Ty sending her senses spiralling dangerously out of control. And it had been far too long since she'd lost control.

This was no ordinary kiss.

Nor was it the power-packed, spur-of-the-moment kiss of the night before.

It was different and she knew that this time she wouldn't be satisfied with anything less than having all of him.

What seemed a mind-blowing eternity later he broke the kiss, pushing her away and staring at her with a slightly shell-shocked expression.

'You're right. Definitely crazy,' she said, reaching across and running her thumb along his bottom lip before she realised what she was doing and snatched her hand away.

'You'll get us arrested,' he muttered, a hint of a smile tugging at the corners of his mouth. 'But, hey, what the hell? With a bit of luck we'd be locked up together and wouldn't that be fun?'

Rather than the heat flooding her body dissipating, it intensified until she thought she'd dissolve unless she got the conversation back on track.

'Look, I take full responsibility for participating in that crazy moment a second ago, but can we get back to why I asked you here?'

She thought he'd block her sidestep.

In fact, she would've bet on it for the old Ty would never have let her get off that easily. Especially considering she'd labelled an explosive kiss a 'crazy moment'.

However, to his credit he let it slip, though the banked heat in his vivid blue eyes had her struggling to string words together.

'Okay. Shoot. What's this favour about?'

'I've got a job for you.'

Surely he wouldn't balk at the idea of an article for the magazine? He knew what her career meant to her. After all, it had been one of the major factors that had driven them apart, their unquenchable thirst to get ahead, to make their mark on the world.

The SEAL and the journalist, taking on the world, and this time around he could help her secure the job of a lifetime, the job that would keep her occupied when he walked out of her life in a week and she tried to forget this amazing man all over again.

It only took a second for the lust in his eyes to blaze again, swift, scorching, irresistible.

'Does it involve being bound to you again?'

Logic fled yet again as her pulse kicked up another notch and she couldn't resist slipping into familiar word games.

'Only if you're very good.'

He stood up and held out his hand. Involuntarily, she took it and he pulled her flush against his body, taking her breath away and sending her heart rate into overdrive all over again.

'Sweetheart, when I'm good, I'm very, very good. And when I'm bad…I'm even better.'

CHAPTER FIVE

KATE had the whole week mapped out.

She'd work from home, gain the relevant information needed to complete the article on the man auction for the magazine while satisfying the intense curiosity about Ty that had been burning within her since she'd first glimpsed his name on the auction list.

Having an inquiring mind was a godsend in her job, but unfortunately the more time she spent with Ty, the more she wanted to know. If anything her curiosity had intensified with every second they spent together and she couldn't concentrate on anything for thoughts of him clouding her mind.

Why was he doing this?

How far would they go to get *reacquainted*?

If those explosive kisses were any indication neither of them would be satisfied with anything less than going the whole way and, while the very idea sent an illicit thrill through her body, she couldn't help but wonder if there was more behind her need to catch up with Ty than curiosity.

The doorbell pealed, interrupting her thoughts and her pulse quickened in anticipation as she was only expecting one person.

Taking a deep breath, she opened the door. 'Didn't take you long to pack.'

He held up a smallish overnight bag and grinned. 'Didn't think I'd need much in the way of clothes.'

Her heart lurched as he leaned against the doorjamb, looking a million bucks and knowing it.

'Come in,' she managed to say, her breath catching as he brushed against her bare arm. 'Minimal clothes, huh? Sounds like we need to have a little chat about your expectations for this week.'

'Hey, I haven't got any expectations. I'm your odd-job man, you call the shots. Simple.'

He glanced around the room, an appreciative gleam in his eyes. 'Nice place you've got here. Not what I expected.'

'What did you expect?'

She'd hoped he'd like her home. For that was what it was to her: a home. Not just bricks and mortar but a place she loved to be. A place that gave her security, a sense of belonging, two things she'd never had growing up with her grumpy, distant mother who'd never really made a home out of their dreary house.

He dropped his bag at the door and stepped inside. 'Guess I expected something different, being Beverly Hills and all.'

'Just because the post code says 90210 doesn't mean I live in a mansion. I'm definitely not movie-star material.'

'I don't know about that.'

A thread of huskiness wove through his voice as his gaze skimmed her body the way it used to: approving, reverent, with a touch of awe in his blue eyes.

Clearing her throat, she turned away before she did something stupid like fling herself at him before he'd even come inside. 'Why don't you make yourself comfortable?'

'How comfortable do you want me to get?'

She stopped mid-stride, forgetting why she'd been heading to the kitchen. 'Consider this place your home for the next week, so whatever makes you happy.'

That was good. She'd managed to deflect his innuendo right back at him.

Predictably, he lobbed straight back. 'These days I usually walk around naked at home.'

Game. Set. Not quite match.

She managed to keep a straight face, barely.

'That works for me. Though I've taken up fencing lately and I have this really weird tendency to practise in my sleep.'

He laughed, the deep sound rippling over her and wrapping her in familiar warmth.

'Thanks for the warning. Though I have to tell you I'm pretty handy with a sword myself.'

His look of assumed innocence backhanded his *coup de grâce* back at her.

Game over. Thank you, linesmen, thank you, ball boys.

She joined in his laughter. 'It's called a rapier in fencing, not a sword. Want a drink?'

'No, thanks.'

She shrugged, wondering why he was still standing around. 'Anything else?'

'I want you.'

Three little words, spoken so quietly that at first she thought she'd imagined them.

'We definitely need to establish house rules,' she said, unable to move even if she'd wanted to as her knees trembled at the sight of Ty strolling towards her.

'I have to kiss you.'

'Ty, I—'

'I have to.'

Tyler's mouth settled over hers and he groaned. He'd ached for this kiss ever since she'd opened the door and he'd seen her standing there wearing a faded purple Lakers T-shirt over cut-off denim shorts, one bare foot propped over the other, a nervous smile playing about her mouth and uncertainty in her hazel eyes, an intoxicating blend of sexy contrasts.

As she responded, her lips opening beneath his, shock slammed into his gut. He didn't just ache for this kiss. He ached for her, to have her in his arms for more than a fleeting minute, maybe for more than a week.

And it scared the hell out of him.

Besides, he couldn't do it to her. She deserved a life and, by the look of her fancy house and snazzy office, she had one now. Being bound to a guy who had no idea what he wanted out of life any more, especially a guy likely to be booted out of the one job he'd known his whole life next week, wasn't for her.

He wouldn't let it happen. She deserved so much better.

Concentrating on the here and now, he slid his hands under her T-shirt and caressed the soft, silky skin beneath, reaching for her breasts that had teased him since he'd walked through the door. Hell, their memory had teased him for the last six years.

'I've missed you,' he murmured against her hair, inhaling the familiar floral fragrance of her shampoo.

Gardenias. He remembered the scent imprinted on his sheets, his pillowcases, his shirts, wherever she'd rested her head.

He grew dizzy at the memory alone and, combined with the touch of her hands fluttering around his waist and the fresh mint taste of her lips, it drove him to the brink of losing control.

'Tell me what you want, Katie,' he murmured before re-capturing her mouth, nibbling and tasting till she made soft, mewing sounds.

This was how he'd imagined it would be from the minute he'd laid eyes on her again.

This was how it should have been for the last six years.

Damn, he'd never felt like this with any other woman. She turned him on with just a look, a flick of her chocolate-brown hair, a glimpse of those amber flecks in her eyes, and for the few glorious moments when she returned his kiss he could ignore the stabbing guilt of the lie he'd told her when he'd walked away six years ago, the constant emptiness of what that had cost him.

Resting her hands on his chest, she gave a slight push, breaking their kiss.

'I want us to take things slow,' she said, raising her eyes slowly to meet his, and the gut-wrenching vulnerability reflected in her hazel depths hit him—hard.

What was he thinking?

It wasn't her fault he kept kissing her whenever he got within two feet and though she responded it didn't mean she wanted some sex-starved SEAL jumping her every time she turned around.

She obviously didn't want *this,* though for the life of him he couldn't figure out what she did want.

His motivations were simple and he'd take whatever fleeting fun she could give him before his world as he knew it was ripped out from under him, but what did she get out of all this?

'Guess you're right about establishing house rules,' he said, thrusting his hands in his pockets to stop from reaching for her again as she tugged her T-shirt down.

She shuffled her bare feet like a recalcitrant schoolchild. 'Where do we start?'

'Ladies first.'

Nodding, she plopped into a comfy armchair, the furthest one away from him, and he sat on the sofa opposite.

Glancing around properly for the first time, he admired the roomy Spanish-style single-storey that exuded a cosiness that sucked him in and would probably spit him out just as quickly.

He didn't belong here.

This was Kate's home, her sanctuary, and he was an intruder, wanting to take whatever scraps of affection she'd throw his way for the next week. For seven days he would put his own needs over hers. Surely no one would begrudge him this interlude considering what he might face next week?

Her eyes pinned him with a knowing stare as if reading his mind and he slipped his poker face into place while his gut churned.

She had the ability to tie him into knots, always had, and right now one thing was for sure: he was way out of his depth. He'd handled that feeling before in the murky waters of the Pacific and Indian Oceans, but on those occasions he'd been trained for it. This time he'd have to survive on instincts alone.

'Go ahead. You're the boss. I'll take my orders from you.'

Confusion flickered in the amber depths of her eyes and he wondered if she felt as off kilter as he did. From the minute they'd hooked up again last night he hadn't been thinking straight and, combined with a sleepless night where he couldn't get her image out of his head, his logic had gone AWOL.

'Okay, house rule one. You look after yourself.'

'Check.'

'House rule two. I'm working on a big article this week so no distractions.'

'Check.'

'House rule three. You need to curb the catching-up behaviour.'

'Such as?'

He bit back a grin, knowing it was cruel to make her spell it out but enjoying the faint blush that stained her cheeks.

She rolled her eyes. 'You kissing me all the time.'

'You've responded.'

She leaped off the sofa as if he'd prodded her with a machine gun and stalked across the room.

'Yeah, well, maybe I've been spending too much time buried in my work so when the first decent guy came along I lost the plot.'

'You think I'm decent, huh?'

He leaned back on the couch, arms outstretched and resting along the top, grinning like a SEAL at graduation.

'I think you're a pain in the ass.'

She flicked her dark hair over her shoulder and recognition washed over him. Even her defence mannerisms hadn't changed in six years.

'And I think you still have a thing for me but, hey, I won't hold it against you.'

Kate couldn't answer for a second. She wanted to argue that he was wrong, that he couldn't be more wrong, but she wouldn't go there. She couldn't, not when her brain was still befuddled by his scintillating kiss.

She had to think logically, to make sure he understood what this week was about. Though apart from his help with the article she was having a hard time figuring out exactly what that was. The lines had blurred around the time he'd laid his hands on her skin and plastered his lips to hers.

She whirled to face him, tucking her hair behind her ears. 'Think whatever you like, though there is something else we need to discuss about this week.'

'Ah…the mysterious favour we didn't quite get around to discussing earlier. Come on, let me have it.'

'I need your help. Your input actually. My chief wants me to do an article on the man auction.'

'Sounds easy enough. Where do I come in?'

If he still valued his privacy as he used to, she knew he wouldn't like the next part. 'Uh, the article's about you and me.'

A tiny frown creased his brow, not detracting from his handsome face one iota. 'What you and me?'

Hearing him say the words out loud hurt more than she could've imagined. Worse still, he was right.

She tilted her head, staring him straight in the eye. 'There isn't any you and me as such, but seeing as we're playing along with this Odd Bod business for the next week, why don't you play along with me on this too?'

He stood up and walked towards her, stopping less than two feet away, invading her personal space with every inch of his incredible body and tipping her chin up, his touch re-igniting the slow burning fuse deep in her heart. 'Play along with what?'

'I need you to be a part of this article. Without your contribution I can't do it.'

'Depends how far I'd have to go?'

'All the way.'

Her statement hung in the air as heat zinged between them, urging her to close the small gap separating them and bury herself in his arms again.

He arched an eyebrow. 'Are we just talking about the article here?'

'What do you think?'

There she went again, unable to bite her tongue, teasing him with innuendo without intending to, half afraid he'd take her up on it, half afraid he wouldn't. What on earth was she doing? She'd just laid down the rules, yet here she was backsliding already. What was wrong with her?

After staring at her with burning desire for five, long, exquisite seconds he shook his head, picked up his car keys from the coffee-table and strode to the door.

'Okay, I'll do it, but right now if I don't get out of here this minute I'm going to blow rule three straight away. I'm kind of addicted to the catching-up behaviour, so I'll put myself out of the way of temptation for a bit. Back soon.'

He blew her a kiss and she scowled as he walked out the door.

Okay, she should be ecstatic he'd agreed to help her, but as the eye-popping memory of the way the denim hugged his butt as he walked out the door refused to budge she knew the week ahead had the potential to blow all their rules sky-high.

* * *

Tyler revved the engine of his Porsche and slid away from the kerb. His baby handled like a dream and provided him with the perfect opportunity to hone his driving skills. After all, no harm in practising what he preached to his charges.

If only handling Kate were as easy. They were on a collision course headed straight for a crash that would probably leave them both nursing emotional injuries that could leave them scarred for life.

Whenever he was near her all he could think about was getting physical and rather than push him away she pushed his buttons more.

He slammed the wheel with the heel of his hand. Kate had always given him all of herself unconditionally and by her eager responses to his kisses it looked as if nothing had changed. Sure, she kept singing the 'no catching up' tune but could she be that detached? Could they be together for the next week and walk away unscathed at the end of it?

Maybe she could. After all, he'd only known her for a few brief months and they'd been apart for six long years. Her new sassy attitude screamed confidence while back then he'd been her touchstone, the guy she'd leaned on when she'd left Australia and landed here with stars in her eyes, hopes of finally getting to know her American grandparents and dreams of making it big in the reporting world. Perhaps the new confident Kate could handle anything?

If she could she was braver than him for he had a sneaking suspicion that the week ahead was going to test him way beyond endurance.

At least she'd come clean about why she wanted him for the week. She needed his help with some stupid article. He'd known she couldn't just want him for his charm and personality.

Heading down Melrose, he wondered if she remembered cruising down this strip with him, checking out the vintage-clothing stores, sharing a hamburger at their favourite diner.

They'd been inseparable for a while and he'd loved showing her the tourist sights like the Mann Theatre, Hollywood Boulevard and day trips to Anaheim to visit Disneyland where they'd laughed like a couple of kids on Space Mountain.

He remembered every carefree day they'd ever had back then and he fully intended to recapture that feeling with his sexy ex over the next week.

Grinning, he angled the car into the orphanage's front gates. Yeah, he'd help her out, but if she expected him to stick to all her rules, particularly the crazy one about keeping his hands off her, she had another thing coming.

The kids were playing beneath an old oak, making enough noise to raise the dead as a flashback had him blinking rapidly—the memory of himself entering these same gates as a terrified youngster.

Nothing much had changed, just the faces passing through, and he'd seen a lot of those over the many years he'd spent here.

A petite woman detached herself from the group and walked towards him as he unfolded his limbs from the car, flexed his knee and stiffened as a wave of excruciating pain stabbed deep and low through the dodgy joint. He should've sold the car years ago but his damn fool pride had stopped him. The way he saw it, the low-slung sports car was the last symbol of his strength. Silly but, hey, it was a guy thing. That and the fact that it was the one luxury he'd ever allowed himself, a hangover from the wishes of a poor kid growing up in the city of dreams.

'Hey, you. Long time no see.'

He held out his arms, knowing that however he was feeling Mary Ramone had the power to make him feel a whole lot better. They'd known each other since they were kids and she knew every one of his moods and he wondered what vibe she'd pick up from him today.

She hugged him before playfully punching his arm. 'Yeah, it's been a while. Work keeping you busy?'

'You know how it is. Teaching those SEALs to handle a vehicle is tough work.'

'Is that why you call it the "crash and bang" course?'

He tweaked her nose. 'CTTC to you civilians, smartypants.'

'Oh, you mean the Countering Terrorist Tactics Course? The one that teaches trainees to use a Browning 9mm, a .38 Special and counter-surveillance techniques? And did I forget to mention the counter-terror driving skills?'

'The girl has a memory.' He clapped and glanced pointedly at the kids. 'Though it's about time you used it for something other than the alphabet.'

She linked her arm through his and guided him towards the decrepit sandstone building he'd once called home. 'I hope you didn't come to lecture me. You know I love my work here.'

'But don't you want to broaden your horizons? See what life holds outside these four walls?'

He sure as hell had wanted to. As soon as he could he'd escaped the orphanage and enrolled in the Navy, eager to travel the world and make it a better place than the one he'd grown up in.

'I love the kids. I can't think of anywhere else I'd rather be than running this place.'

'Yeah, but you've spent your whole life here,' he persisted, knowing his advice fell on deaf ears but compelled to continue anyway. 'If we had more money, someone else could run it and you'd be free to pursue anything you wanted.'

A worried expression crossed her face and the knife of guilt embedded in his conscience twisted. He'd left as soon as he could, Mary hadn't and she'd forfeited her life's dreams while he had fulfilled his.

'We do need more cash and soon. Otherwise, these gates

will close permanently. I'll be out on the streets, not to mention the poor little tykes.'

'Isn't there something else we can do?'

She reached up and smoothed the frown from his forehead. 'You do enough.'

He continued as if he hadn't heard her. 'We need to raise the profile of this place, raise people's awareness…'

He trailed off as a smidgeon of an idea hatched in his mind, growing from chick-size to pterodactyl in a second.

'Want a drink?'

Mary bustled around the kitchen, preparing dinner for the children. She'd always looked after him like this from the first day he'd set foot in the orphanage all those years ago. She was a mere eleven months older than him yet she'd mothered him as though the age difference were eleven years and he loved her for it.

He shook his head. 'No, thanks. Look, I have to run. See you soon.'

He dropped a kiss on the top of her head and strode out the door, ignoring her protest of 'But you just got here.'

He had a plan and the sooner he put it to Kate, the better.

Kate lit the final candle and stepped back from the table. So she'd pulled out all stops tonight, but she had a feeling she was going to need all the help she could get.

No matter how much she deluded herself that the week ahead was all part of her job and might provide some light-hearted fun in her workaholic world, she knew deep down that there would come a time very soon where she'd cross the line, throw herself at Ty and there'd be no turning back.

Her almost frantic responses to his kisses proved it.

She wanted him. Badly. Insanely. Desperately.

She couldn't get him out of her head and having him here for a week would be more temptation than she could withstand. More than she wanted to withstand if she was completely honest with herself. What had she been thinking laying down those rules? No catching up—who was she kidding? She wanted to *catch up* with him in a bad way.

And why not?

It shouldn't be a big deal. She was a career girl with high aspirations who lived life to the full. Why couldn't she take what Ty offered and say bye-bye in a week?

It would be so much fun to explore the unresolved tension between them, to see if they still combusted the way they used to. But was she immune to him emotionally? She'd got over him a long time ago but spending one-on-one time could be dangerous.

Could she let him go at the end of the week if they clicked as she expected? They'd already picked up where they'd left off mentally, matching each other quip for quip, teasing, pushing the boundaries. What if the sex was as good as she remembered—or, worse, better?

Was she strong enough to get over him a second time?

Well, there was only one way to find out.

Glancing around, she fiddled with the place settings for the umpteenth time, making sure everything was perfect. Dimmed Tiffany lamps sent muted light over the room, making the candles seem so much brighter. The table setting for two appeared cosier with candles, the shadows cast creating an intimacy that beckoned, reflecting off the coffee-coloured walls, deepening the rich ochre of the sofa and high-lighting the turquoise cushions scattered in a casual formation.

Ty would probably laugh his head off if he remembered how they'd shared their meals all those years ago and compared it to this fancy setting. Back then they'd eaten pizza out of a box most nights courtesy of her complete lack of culinary skills, and rarely at the table, preferring the cosiness of cuddling in bed licking mozzarella off each other's fingers before turning their attentions to other parts.

The memory brought a smile to her face and before she could uncork the wine the doorbell rang. Wiping her sweaty palms on a napkin, she smoothed her skirt and opened the door.

'Hi. Care for something to eat?'

She aimed for casual yet her voice came out husky as her pulse galloped at the look in Ty's eye.

'I should warn you. I'm ravenous.'

His intense gaze started at her toes and worked its way slowly upward, leaving her in little doubt that he wanted to start at dessert.

And come back for seconds.

CHAPTER SIX

TYLER thought he knew Kate but the minute she opened the door wearing a slip of material parading as a dress she blew every preconception he'd ever had.

When he'd left earlier with a smart-ass remark about not sticking to rule number three he could've sworn she'd wanted to flay him alive. He'd seen it in the glowing gold flecks of her eyes, in the bunched fists, in the clenched jaw. He could read body language a mile away and hers had screamed, 'Back off.'

So what was with the vamp dress?

Soft blue material clung to every inch of her delicious curves, ending just above her knee and wrapped halter-style around her neck. It tied at exactly the spot he'd wanted to plant his lips the minute she'd sauntered up on stage to join him last night.

If she wanted to tempt him, to drive him wild, to send him to the doc at the base for debriefing, she was certainly going about it the right way.

Rules? What rules? It appeared Kate had a penchant for teasing and the way he was feeling he'd be lucky to last the next minute without shooting down her stupid rules in flames.

'You look amazing. Did you dress up for me?'

'Only if you're lucky, sailor boy. Want some wine?'

'Please. Mind if I take a quick shower?'

She waved towards the back of the house. 'Go right ahead. I put your bag in the spare room, second door on the left. Towels are in the bathroom.'

So much for the faint hope she was planning on going through with her 'going the whole way' taunt. He'd looked forward to waking up next to her despite the fact she'd laid down clear cohabiting rules for the week.

Who was he trying to kid? He'd been counting on it. Instead, he'd be closeted in the spare room, tossing and turning and dreaming of his sexy ex across the hall.

'Thanks,' he said, admiring her long, bare legs accentuated by sexy black shoes with monstrous heels before heading for the shower. A long, cold shower.

He didn't get it.

If Kate was so keen on sticking to rules why was she sending him mixed messages? She responded to his kisses, she joined in his flirtatious banter and now this cosy dinner scenario with her looking like a walking, talking fantasy.

He didn't know what to think, let alone how to respond. Some of the tougher missions he'd faced had been a walk in the park compared with figuring out what made her tick these days.

Kate waited till Ty left the room before sinking into a chair with a glass of wine in hand.

She'd failed.

So much for giving him an obvious sign she was willing to throw rule three out the window and go for it.

He'd obviously liked her outfit, but as for making a fuss about being in the spare room he'd shrugged it off, not appearing to be bothered in the slightest. She'd expected him to make some cutesy remark. Heck, she'd hoped he'd pick up his bag and march straight into her bedroom.

Now she'd have to tell him what she wanted, and how embarrassing would that be?

'Oh, by the way, Ty, remember my hands-off rule? Well, scratch that. I've actually still got the hots for you so why don't we spend the next few days getting reacquainted in every way?'

Yeah, as if she could say that.

Darn it, why was this so difficult? She had no trouble being assertive in the business arena; why couldn't she just tell Ty what she wanted?

It wasn't as if the guy were immune to her. After all, he'd kissed her several times over the last twenty-four hours and flirted incessantly.

Hating her indecision, she tried to ignore the sound of the running shower by turning up the CD player. Unfortunately, once she'd heard the taps turn the image of Ty naked with water sluicing down his toned body sprang to mind and she couldn't dislodge it.

Sipping her wine, she focussed on the soft jazz filtering through the room, though the alcohol and music didn't help. Before she knew it she'd emptied the glass and was still tuned to the sound of running water rather than soulful sax. Leaning back in the chair, she closed her eyes for a moment.

'You work too hard.'

Ty strolled into the room looking delectable in bone-coloured chinos and a casual white shirt open at the neck. The sandalwood soap she kept for guests had been put to good use if the heady scent emanating off him was any in-dication and she breathed deeply, infusing her senses with it, with him.

'Occupational hazard,' she said, trying not to focus on the tanned V visible at the base of his throat, the area of skin she knew drove him crazy when nibbled on.

Damn memories…

She tried to relax as he rested his hands on her shoulders and slowly stroked and kneaded the knots in her neck muscles, and though she knew his touch was therapeutic the feel of his warm hands on her bare skin sent erotic shivers down her spine.

'I'm pretty tense,' she murmured, leaning her head forward to allow him better access.

How long since she'd had a massage, done something indulgent or just plain taken time out for herself? Too long if her reaction to Ty's touch was anything to go by, though she knew that probably had more to do with who was giving her the massage than the rub itself.

'Just relax.'

He increased the pressure, his thumbs circling into the base of her skull, and she stifled a loud groan of pleasure.

'Ooh…yeah. Right there.'

His hands stilled and she realised how her words sounded. Aiming for light-hearted, she said, 'I didn't tell you to stop.'

'Yes, boss.'

Kate couldn't think straight as his thumbs started stroking the indentations above her collar-bones, rhythmic circles that enticed rather than soothed, liquid heat seeping through her body and turning her bones to mush.

'How do you know all the right spots?'

'Your body speaks volumes.' He wound his way back to her neck, his gentle yet firm touch hypnotising.

'So what do you think it's telling you now?'

Her breath caught as his fingers snagged on the tie of her dress and she wished she hadn't had that glass of wine on an empty stomach. The alcohol had taken the edge off her nerves, given her false courage, and there was no telling what she'd say next.

'The suggestions your body makes, it should be branded with an "R" rating.'

As if to emphasise the fact, he lifted the halter knot at the base of her neck and kissed her, so softly that at first she thought she'd imagined it.

'You're incredible, Katie, but I don't want to be accused

of breaking rules again, and on my first day too,' he murmured against her ear, his breath soft and warm.

Her head snapped up as he walked to the table, her body missing his touch so much it bordered on physical pain, her brain unable to process how he could switch off like that when a second ago he'd seemed about to untie her dress and have his way with her.

'Nice set-up. What's for dinner?'

He pulled out a chair and looked in her direction, a knowing smile flirting around his mouth as if he could read her mind.

Struggling to keep her tone casual, she said, 'Spaghetti marinara. Salad. Nothing too flash.'

Thanks to her bones having dissolved under his expert hands she almost staggered to the table, kicking off her high heels in the process. So much for the illusion of longer legs. At this point she'd settle for both legs staying vertical rather than sprawling on the floor.

'What's so funny?'

He chuckled, a pure happy sound that evoked instant memories of how much they used to laugh together, how much fun they'd had in their too-brief relationship. 'Still a one-glass wonder, I see. Take a seat. I'll get dinner.'

She sank gratefully into the chair as he pushed it towards the table and she avoided the wine bottle. She'd had more than enough for one night.

Besides, if she were to pluck up the courage to tell him exactly how badly she had the hots for him she wanted to remember if they got to the fun stuff later.

'Nice manners. You must've had a good teacher.'

'One of the best.' He strolled into the kitchen, tension etched into the breadth of his shoulders.

Funnily enough, he'd never mentioned family six years ago and she hadn't asked, being so rapt in the throes of first love. In fact, he'd skilfully avoided any questions regarding his childhood, and she knew next to nothing about the man she'd loved apart from the fact he had been raised in LA, how he liked his eggs in the mornings, what side of the bed he liked to sleep on and how many times a night he could please her.

Resisting the urge to fan her flushed cheeks—memories of Ty's prowess in bed combined with wine were not conducive to staying cool—she said, 'Did your mum teach you?'

Silence greeted her question, soon followed by the sounds of pots opening and clanking spoons.

'Ty?'

'No.'

He strode towards the table, bearing plates heaped with steaming pasta and seafood sauce.

'Then who?'

He ignored her once again as he strode towards the kitchen, this time returning with the salad.

'What's with the twenty questions?'

She shrugged, as if his answer weren't important.

'Just wondering. We didn't exactly do lots of talking six years ago.'

She twirled a few lengths of spaghetti onto her fork and managed to shovel them into her mouth, avoiding his eyes the whole time, wondering if her veiled reference to what they had spent their time on might give her the opening to say what she wanted now.

'You're right about that.'

His voice was strangely flat and she sneaked a peek, not surprised to see him concentrating on his pasta as if it hid the answer to world peace.

Taking a deep breath, she plunged in. 'Maybe this is a good opportunity for us to, you know, talk? For old times' sake, see how far we've come.'

He lifted his head, his blue-eyed gaze meeting her dead-on.

'You know what that sounds like?' he asked archly.

She nodded, knowing the rising blush staining her cheeks would be a dead give-away if her leaning so far forward and practically climbing onto his lap wasn't enough of a clue.

'Uh-huh.' Managing a smile, she pointed to her dress. 'Guess I kind of hoped this would be enough of a sign that I'm not so rigid on the rules, but you didn't take the hint so maybe I'll have to spell it out for you.'

His eyes blazed with instant heat before he blinked and reached across the table to capture her hands.

'You don't need to spell anything out. I know you want me as much as I want you. But are you sure? Come the end of this week I'm out of your life. Are you absolutely certain you want to concentrate on here and now?'

Oh, yeah.

She didn't want to think beyond this week, she just wanted for seven days to let her hair down for once and have a little fun with the sexiest man she'd ever known. However, hearing Ty casually stating that their reunion was a one-week-only deal hurt like the devil and it shouldn't.

Damn it, she wanted it that way.

She just didn't need reminding of the fact.

'I'm sure,' she murmured, squeezing his hands, hoping he could read the excitement in her eyes as anticipation blazed a trail through her body.

Shaking his head, he sat back, confusion warring with desire on his face.

'I'll be honest with you, Katie. I don't get this. We both made a conscious decision to end our relationship six years ago. We had careers to forge, places to go, things to do. Then you turn up out of the blue, buy me at some crazy male auction, tell me to take a hike, then change your mind and we've barely kept our hands off each other ever since. What's going on? Do you really think you'll be happy with just a week-long fling?'

Sighing, she disengaged her hands from his and reached for her wineglass. One more sip for courage wouldn't hurt.

'You want the truth? I'm married to my job. I haven't dated in a while. I'm stale, stifled. Then I saw your name on the auction list; I got curious. I thought we could catch up over a drink. Then I had too much champagne, went a little crazy and bought you, tried to fob you off before agreeing to have you trail after me for a week, and here we are.'

His stare didn't waver and she wondered yet again if he could still read her like a book. He'd had a happy knack of doing it back then, honing in on her thoughts with startling clarity. However, this time he'd come up blank because she'd basically told him the truth. Well, most of it anyway.

'So you're bored and you want to have a little fun? And that's it?'

She nodded, hating the logical, cut-and-dried way they were discussing this when he should be clearing the table in one swoop and bending her over it to have his wicked way with her.

'In a nutshell, yes.'

After a few seconds' silence where she felt like the biggest fool in the world for laying her cards on the table, he smiled and shook his head.

'You haven't changed a bit. You never ceased to surprise me back then and it looks like nothing has changed.'

Filled with an indescribable joy that she'd spilt her guts and he hadn't laughed at her—in fact, in a roundabout way he'd agreed to give her what she wanted—she picked up her fork and toyed with her pasta, feigning nonchalance.

'Oh, I think you'd be surprised. I may have changed in all sorts of interesting ways.'

'Is that so?'

His eyes narrowed to slivers of fiery blue as heat flared between them in an instant and she laid her fork down, her appetite vanishing. She couldn't eat when he looked at her like that, as if he'd like to gobble her up rather than the meal she'd prepared.

'Uh-huh, but maybe you should finish dinner? You know, to keep up your strength?'

She had to lighten the mood, say something, anything, to distract herself from the insane desire to clamber onto his lap and ravish him.

'Nothing wrong with my endurance, you should know that,' he said, grinning like a guy who knew exactly how impressive his capacities were in that department.

Struggling to keep a straight face, she said, 'Yeah, but you're older now, probably more decrepit. Maybe a healthy serving of pasta will boost your energy levels.'

Rather than Tyler laughing out loud as she expected, a flicker of unease flashed across his face and she wondered what he'd faced in the line of duty and what changes it might have wrought on him emotionally as well as physically.

'You're right about the decrepit part. Since my knee blew jumping out of a helicopter and I had it reconstructed, I haven't been the same since.'

'I was only kidding,' she said, hating the serious turn their conversation had taken, wishing she'd kept things light-hearted.

The flicker of unease had turned into a sombre expression, with his eyes hooded in mystery.

'Being an instructor just isn't the same as active duty,' he said, almost to himself as he picked up his wineglass and took a healthy sip. 'But, hey, you don't want to hear boring tales of battle-scarred Navy guys, right?'

'I'm interested in hearing about what you've been up to,' she said, hoping he'd open up more to her now than he had six years ago.

Back then he'd been tight-lipped about his job, his training, preferring to concentrate on making her laugh rather than revealing what drove him to take on one of the most dangerous and highly skilled jobs in the world.

He clicked his fingers. 'Speaking of work, I need to ask you for a favour. You know that article about you and me? Well, I'll answer all your questions if you run an article on the orphanage. A big spread. Full coverage. High exposure.'

She sat up, surprised at the swift change of topic, but grateful his expression had lightened up.

'Are you serious?'

His interest in the orphanage was a lot more than he had initially let on and she wondered what was behind it.

'Deadly. Think you can do it?'

'Why?'

'It's personal.'

In a blinding flash of clarity, Kate knew it had to involve a woman. What else could it be? Just because she'd been dateless for a while didn't mean he had. After all, look at the guy. What woman could resist?

She shouldn't care; she really shouldn't.

But she did. And the surprising ache in the vicinity of her heart told her just how much.

She decided to call his bluff, following a masochistic urge to find out more about this cause that meant so much to him— or, more realistically, who was behind it.

'I need to check it out first, see if it's newsworthy. Why don't you take me out there tomorrow?'

'Sounds good.' He picked up his fork and stabbed it into his pasta till it stood vertically. 'Now, maybe I should get back to eating? You know, to keep up my strength and all.'

Kate smiled, though inside her mind churned.

She'd thought she'd had it all a few moments ago with Ty agreeing to a week of fun. But his unorthodox request had taken some of the gloss off what had promised to be the most fun she'd had in ages.

Ty had a life that didn't involve her and suddenly the truth hit home.

She didn't really know this man. She never had.

And a week just wasn't enough to play catch-up.

Not the way she wanted.

CHAPTER SEVEN

KATE pointed at Ty's car and grinned. 'Nice wheels.'

'It's just a Porsche.'

His answering little-boy grin told her exactly how much he loved his car as he opened the passenger door, resurrecting memories of his perfect manners and the way he'd made her feel like a queen. Not many guys did that any more and she liked it. She might be independent and self-sufficient, but she hadn't burned all her bras just yet.

'Yeah, just a Porsche. So what if it's sleek, powerful and built for speed, right?'

His smile widened as he gunned the engine. 'Sounds a bit like me. Apart from the speed thing. I prefer to take things nice and slow.'

She quirked an eyebrow. 'Could've fooled me, the way you've been carrying on.'

No matter how hard she tried she couldn't get the memory of his scorching kisses out of her head. Not that she was trying particularly hard to forget.

Ty concentrated on the road so she couldn't read the expression in his eyes. 'Have we made love yet?'

'No,' she mumbled, heat flooding her cheeks at his typical blunt assessment of the situation.

'See, told you. Slow.'

She barely caught his murmured addition, 'Too bloody slow.'

A flood of heat flowed through her body at the delicious recollection of exactly how slow Ty could take things.

He'd been a master lover, knowing exactly how to please her, to make her want him so much she couldn't think straight. First loves were supposed to be like that, a bit over the top, surreal, almost too good to be true, and she wondered if he'd changed.

Would he still be a great lover?

The thought notched up her temperature another few degrees and she clasped her hands firmly together, suppressing the urge to lean over and stroke his thigh.

She loved him in jeans, the denim hugging in all the right places, leaving little to her already over-stimulated imagination. She'd lain awake all night tossing and turning in her bed while less than twenty feet away had slept her sexy ex. The same ex who flirted whenever he got within two feet of her, the same ex who made her lose sight of the fact he'd be out of her life by the end of this week whenever he talked in that low, husky voice or looked at her with hunger in his blue eyes.

Their dinner had ended on a surprisingly chaste note after her true confessions but in a way she'd been relieved. It had been one hell of a day: seeing Ty first thing, lunch at Venice Beach, having him move in and dinner had left her more drained than she could've imagined.

'Your house is great. It feels like a real home.'

'My grandparents built it when they first married. Apparently they were both actors in Hollywood's early days and nothing's been done to it since then. That's why it's modest by Beverly Hills standards.'

'I like it. It's comfortable, the type of place that feels good to hang out in.'

His praise thrilled her more than it should. Why should she care what he thought of her home? He'd waltz out of it in a week without looking back.

'Thanks. I've felt like that from the minute I stepped into it.'

She'd loved living with her grandparents, the feisty old couple who had fought and made up till their dying day. They'd showered her with love and affection for the brief period they'd known each other.

'How did you meet up with your grandparents?'

'After we split up, I looked them up. I barely knew my dad, who preferred going walkabout in the outback to living in Sydney with his family, and have little to thank him for except that through him I was entitled to American citizenship. But, I knew his parents lived in Beverly Hills so I checked out the phone book, called them and they welcomed me with open arms. I lived with them for a while till they both passed away within a few months of each other.'

Her voice shook at the memory. For some reason, most of the people she loved died or left her and, though she'd come to terms with her loss a while ago, seeing Ty again and knowing she'd lose him in a week ripped open old wounds she'd thought long healed.

'Sorry seems pretty inadequate right about now.'

Ty turned to face her as the car slid to a stop. Compassion shone from his eyes and she was surprised to see something else: empathy.

She'd almost say he knew what it felt like to be shunned by parents, to yearn for love so badly you could almost taste it.

Glancing around, she noted the orphanage's rickety gates, the ancient oak tree, the crumbling stone building, and with a startling flash of insight she knew. A piece of knowledge she'd long forgotten, in fact had barely known, suddenly clicking into place.

This was why he'd dedicated his week off.

This was why he wanted her to feature an article on the place.

'You grew up here, didn't you?'

He nodded, his expression closed, before unfolding his

long legs from behind the wheel. 'Come on. Time to meet the kids and Mary.'

Mary.

Kate's initial relief that Ty's past was motivation for his interest in the orphanage faded as she watched in growing horror as he strode towards a stunning woman standing on the front steps and enveloped her in a hug.

She'd never seen anyone so delicate, so pretty. Long black hair framed a heart-shaped face, the outstanding feature a pair of intense green eyes. The woman couldn't have been more than five-two, had curves in all the right places, giving the impression of a china doll, and Kate could understand why Ty would want to pick up the porcelain princess and cradle her.

Hating the shaft of jealousy stabbing her, Kate waited till they pulled apart before approaching and holding out her hand.

'Hi. I'm Kate Hayden, a friend of Tyler's.'

'Mary Ramone. Nice to meet you.' The doll's handshake was firm, warm. 'Please come inside. Tyler's told me all about you.'

Kate winced, knowing that couldn't be true. Mary obviously had no idea she'd been so desperate for a little fun in her life that she'd stooped so low as to purchase her ex at a male auction.

'Tyler rang me first thing this morning and said you're doing a story on the orphanage? That's great.' Mary sliced freshly baked carrot cake, judging by the delicious aroma filling the kitchen, and set a percolator for coffee, her soft smile warm and friendly the entire time.

A regular little homebody too.

Stifling her bitchy side, Kate deliberately kept her answer noncommittal. 'I'm looking into it. I thought I'd check out the orphanage today and run it past my boss. He makes the final decisions as to what stories the magazine does.'

If it meant that she would have to spend more time at the

orphanage seeing Ty and Mary playing best pals hell would freeze over before *Femme* ran an article on the place.

Ty interrupted. 'Surely your input is valued, though? If you say the story is appropriate, your boss would agree?'

Reluctantly, she nodded. 'It shouldn't be a problem, though all he seems to care about at the moment is the feature on the man auction. However, we can possibly tie the two stories together.'

Mary laughed. 'I heard about that. You're a brave lady, Kate, buying this guy for a week. Good luck.'

Suddenly, shame washed through Kate. Mary seemed like a genuinely nice person. It wasn't her fault that a green-eyed monster the size of Disneyland resided in Kate's head. Or was that her heart?

'Oh, I think I can handle him.'

The man in question merely raised an eyebrow.

Mary dropped an affectionate kiss on the top of his head and Kate's heart clenched, the pain almost visceral. 'I tried looking after him for years and it didn't get me anywhere.'

Kate subdued her aching heart and tried to make polite conversation. 'So you two grew up together?'

Mary nodded. 'Yeah and he was a terror. Still is, if you ask me.'

Ty swatted her butt as she walked past. 'No one's asking you, pest.'

That did it. The sight of his hand on Mary's cute little butt even for one second was one second too long for her.

'Can we look around now? I need to pitch the idea to Henry as soon as possible if the article's to make this week's deadline.' She forced a smile when in fact she felt physically ill.

'Sure. Follow me.'

Mary led the way and Kate felt like an ogre in munchkin land as she followed the petite woman.

Why had she thought Ty could even be remotely interested

in a five-ten giant when he could have cabbage-patch cute?
Not that she wanted his interest beyond this week. Right?

She repeated the silent question as Mary led her through
the orphanage and introduced her to the children. Their
cherubic faces almost broke her heart; that was, if it hadn't
already sustained a few blows back in the kitchen.

In under an hour she'd seen enough. The orphanage would
make a great human-interest story for *Femme*'s readers.

As they walked back to the car Kate made mental notes
about the orphanage, anything to keep her mind occupied
and off the topic of Ty and Mary.

Were they involved?

Had they ever been involved?

*Did she really think she could have a week with Ty and
walk away at the end?*

'Thanks for the tour, Mary. Nice meeting you.'

'You too. I'm looking forward to seeing what you come
up with for the article. And if you need anything else don't
hesitate to call.'

Kate mumbled a vague goodbye and slid into the car, studiously avoiding watching any departing contact between Ty
and Mary. No way was she a glutton for punishment.

As Ty backed the car out of the driveway her words fell out
in a rush. 'I'm not sure if I can do the story.'

'What?'

'It may not work.'

Ty's hands clenched the wheel and his gaze fixed on the
road but she could read the signs. Not happy.

'Why not?'

'Just trust me on this one, okay?'

He would have to because there was no way she could tell
him the real reason.

'No.'

He paused for a moment and she tensed, ready for an

argument as he continued. 'Is this some strange jealousy thing on your part? Because I saw the way you looked at Mary and it's totally unnecessary. Mary's like a sister to me.'

How did he do that, read her mind as if it were an open book? Surely six years' absence should've dulled it?

Sister, huh? Sure.

'You're way off base. The world doesn't revolve around you. Besides, I'd have to care to be jealous.'

'Yeah, and your point is?'

'I don't care.'

She expected thunder and a bolt of lightning to strike her down. Or her nose to grow at least another three inches.

'Sure you do, Pinocchio.'

Damn, he'd done it again. The mental telepathy thing he had going on was really starting to annoy her.

She crossed her arms, digging her nails into her upper arms, and her mouth twitched as she remembered doing the same thing years ago whenever she'd stood her ground around him.

'I'm just not sure about the story, okay? Let's leave it at that.'

'No story, no Tyler.'

'Pardon?'

'You need me…for your article.'

He'd left a sufficient pause to insinuate just how he thought she needed him.

She swore softly. He was right, on both counts.

'So what's it to be? My full co-operation in exchange for a story on the orphanage?'

Unfortunately, she had a fair idea what his full co-operation would involve. Which was totally outrageous and yet…

'I don't like being blackmailed.'

He chuckled. 'It's a deal, then. So, when should we get started?'

She didn't know if he meant on the interview, the story or the co-operation.

'I hate it when you're cocky.'

He pulled into her driveway before answering, his blue eyes sparking with the knowledge that he had the upper hand.

'No. You just hate it when I'm right.'

In response, she sent him a haughty glare and slammed the car door. Not that she was particularly annoyed with him when she was the one acting like a jealous schoolgirl.

Logically, she knew there hadn't been the slightest sign of flirtation between Ty and Mary, and even if there had been she had no right to feel this way.

Ty was her past. Just because she had him in her life again for a week didn't mean she owned him. Far from it. He'd always been his own man, independent to the nth degree, and she'd been the same way. They'd parted on civil terms so why was she going all mushy now?

Damn it, this business wasn't turning out the way she'd hoped. What happened to having fun? She needed to lighten up, a lot.

'When are you going to start obeying me like a good Odd Bod should?'

Unlocking the front door and punching in the alarm code, she entered the room, grateful for the familiar rush that enveloped her whenever she came home. No matter how busy or crazy her life got, she always had the comfort of this place.

Ty brushed past her, the soft cotton of his T-shirt scraping against the bare skin on her arm and sending an unexpected tingle racing through her. Taking a seat on the couch, he laid his arms across the back of it and crossed his ankles, long denim-clad legs stretched out in front in a typical, casual, 'I'm in control' pose.

'When hell freezes over.'

To top it off he grinned, that infuriating, sexy smile that notched up the heat all over again.

She stared, unsure whether to kiss him or throw the nearest thing handy, which happened to be an expensive antique vase. Instead, she took a deep breath and walked towards the kitchen.

'Where are you going? Tired of playing already?'

She didn't break stride. She wouldn't give him the satisfaction. Especially when laughter bubbled up within and she almost snorted trying to control it.

'No. Just stocking up on ice blocks, turning up the air-conditioning and ordering a blizzard.'

His warm chuckles wrapped around her, a comforting sound that never failed to raise a smile.

'That's it. Crank up the cold treatment. Not that it's going to do you any good.'

'Want to make a bet?'

She stopped in the doorway and turned to face him, wondering how far she could push him, wondering if this time their banter would lead where she'd wanted it to from the first minute she'd laid eyes on him again, with her cocooned in his arms and his body doing incredible things to hers.

'I'm a SEAL, remember? I can handle anything you care to dish out.'

'Big statement. But can you deliver?'

Ty didn't move a muscle, but she could see the tension in his bulging biceps as he surreptitiously gripped the back of the sofa and the swift flare of fire in his eyes as they darkened to midnight.

Taking a deep breath, knowing this was it, she murmured, 'Dare you.'

He leaped off the couch and walked towards her, sending her new-found seductive powers spiralling out of control as she inadvertently backed away till the breakfast counter digging into her back stopped her short.

Heart pounding with excitement, fear and trepidation, she said the first thing that came into her head. 'How about a swim first?'

'So what I'm hearing is that you want us to get our gear off and get wet?'

His eyes gleamed with challenge and, damn him, he knew she would never back away from one.

They'd always been like this: fiery, spontaneous, playful and challenging. Always trying to get the better of the other, always playing the game, trying to outwit the other.

Well, time to resurrect old times and have her fun in the process.

She tilted her head up, determined to stare him down. 'Yeah, that's exactly what I want.'

He smiled and ran one finger lightly down her bare arm, sending fireworks shooting through her body and liquid heat pooling in all the right places.

'Be careful what you wish for, Katie.'

'Why? Think you can make all my dreams come true?'

She managed to stay upright as his finger slid up her arm, across her collar-bone and towards her ear lobe in agonising slowness.

'I'm here to do whatever you want me to.' He tapped the end of her nose and smiled. 'Me the Odd Bod, you the boss, remember? Meet you out the back in a minute.'

She stared as he turned and strutted out of the kitchen, leaving her hot and trembling and wanting him more than ever.

CHAPTER EIGHT

OKAY, so this hadn't been one of her smarter ideas. When she'd suggested they take a swim she'd imagined cooling off a tad before she took the plunge with Ty in more ways than one.

However, she should've known better. If the thought of Ty wearing nothing but trunks was enough to send her body into meltdown, what hope did she have when confronted with the real thing?

As if on cue he strutted out to the pool, dropped his towel on the nearest chair, flashed a cocky smile and stepped into the water. She'd expected him to execute a fancy dive into the deep end, but it looked as if his knee, which he unconsciously rubbed or flexed at times, must be giving him more trouble than he let on.

'Come on in. The water's great.'

He trod water as his gaze slid over her body, starting at her toes and slowly working its way up, leaving a trail of super-sensitised skin as if he'd physically touched her.

'Nice bikini you're almost wearing.'

He grinned and dived under the water before she could reply, not that she could've given him a coherent response if she'd tried.

The way he'd looked at her, with adoration, with desire, had her insides tied up in knots along with her tongue.

Not that she'd said much of anything since he'd strolled out to the pool, every rippling muscle on display. She'd feasted her eyes, memorising every line and plane of his body to savour and dissect later. Washboard abs, moulded pecs, lean yet hard legs. All that a girl could ask for and he was freestyling in her pool, inviting her in. What was she waiting for?

She knew.

She knew that the minute she entered the water any last semblance of self-control would exit her mind. If they so much as touched, skin to skin, without the flimsy barrier of clothes she'd lose it.

Wasn't that what she wanted?

Her body screamed yes while her heart reserved its better judgment.

This wasn't just a casual fling.

This was her ex she was considering making love with.

And though they'd both made it clear they wanted nothing more at the end of the week, she was scared.

Scared of her memories, scared of how he made her feel, scared of wanting too much and most of all scared of falling for him all over again.

Damn it, why couldn't she let go of her inhibitions and enjoy the week as two friends getting reacquainted before moving on?

Because this was Ty she was talking about and she knew what would happen if she dropped her guard altogether.

She'd spent a lifetime playing it safe thanks to her overprotective mother, and though she'd escaped Doris's influence years ago she still found herself making the right decisions all the time, the conservative choices.

Maybe just this once she could do the opposite?

Bracing herself, she muttered, 'Ready or not, here I come,' and stepped into the tepid water, knowing she was far from ready but willing to take the plunge anyway.

Tyler surfaced in time to watch Kate step into the water.

He'd hoped a lazy five laps would take the edge off his hunger but it hadn't. He'd been aroused the minute he'd spotted her in that barely there bikini, the black triangles held together by flimsy string. One tug and all that lushness could spill into his waiting hands.

Kate had always been temptation personified but the beautiful young woman she'd been had blossomed into a sexy siren and he had to answer her call.

Yeah, she was pure temptation, all right. She'd been toying with him since the auction and it was time to put an end to it. He was a SEAL not a Boy Scout. She'd pushed all his buttons and he couldn't hold out any longer.

Time to see if his smart-mouthed ex stood by her word.

'You were right. The water feels great.'

She hadn't moved far from the steps as if poised for flight and he knew he'd have to take the lead. Not that it bothered him. Taking charge was what he did best.

However, as much as he wanted Kate, and he pretty much knew she wanted him as badly, a small part of him wished she'd make the first move just as she had all those years ago.

'Come in. You'll love it.'

Their eyes locked and he saw her pupils dilate, whether in shock or anticipation he didn't know.

This was it, the moment when she'd flee or stay. God, he wanted her, more than ever.

Suddenly, it happened.

She submerged beneath the water for several seconds and swam towards him, and when she finally stood before him, water sluicing down her luscious body, he couldn't speak.

If his life went belly-up after this week he'd remember this moment for all eternity, treasuring the sight of the gorgeous woman he'd once been lucky enough to share a relationship with staring at him with tentative longing in her expressive hazel eyes.

'Hope you didn't burn up too much energy with all those laps.'

She smiled, a slow, upward turning of her lips that undid him completely and he growled as he reached for her, pulling her close.

'I'm trained for stamina. I was just getting warmed up.'

She wrapped her legs around him, just stopping short of bringing her intimate heat in contact with him, and he gritted his teeth, barely able to restrain himself from tearing off the flimsy barrier of cloth between them and taking her on the spot.

'So, are you?'

In response, he pulled her flush against him, almost groaning aloud as she rubbed against him. 'What does it feel like to you?'

She looped her arms around his neck and snuggled closer. 'I'd say warm-up's over and it's time for the main game to start.'

He stared at her, mesmerised by the glowing gold flecks in her eyes, by the heat that shimmered and flared in her irises.

She'd always been so responsive, so eager, and in a flash he knew he'd missed her more than he'd let himself believe all these years.

Unable to resist a second longer he slanted his mouth over hers, amazed at the instant response of her lips, putting every ounce of feeling into the kiss.

Like the few times they'd kissed already he combusted in an instant, his control shredded as he wanted to devour her, to taste her, to examine every inch of her exquisite body with his hands and his mouth and his tongue.

He cupped her butt as she rocked her hips against him, inflaming the burning heat sizzling between them.

'Ty, I want—'

'I know, Katie. I want you too.'

More than was rational. More than was sane.

He shouldn't want her this much, need her this much.

They were over at the end of this week. His head believed it; the rest of him had some serious catching up to do.

The water lapped around them as he waded towards the steps, eager to get inside quickly before the last of his self-control vanished and he took her here and now without protection.

As he strode towards the house Kate wiggled against him and he cupped her butt tighter.

'Do you have a thing for my ass?' she whispered in his ear, her teasing tongue flicking around his ear lobe.

'Sweetheart, I have a thing for *all* of you.'

He gently squeezed, bringing her in closer contact to the evidence of how much of a thing he had for her, knowing that whatever happened with his career next week, whatever happened with the rest of his life, he'd never regret getting together with Kate again.

She was worth it, every special inch of her.

Kate clung to Ty, her skin on fire. She had trouble breathing with his hands splayed across her butt, holding her so close their bodies were plastered together.

Memories came flooding back, overwhelming in their intensity as she remembered the first time he'd held her like this, the first time he'd undressed her, the first time they'd touched skin to skin.

She would've done anything to have him back then. In a way she had, going as far as proposing to him to hang onto the magic they'd created.

But that had been plain silly. They'd both been too young, too driven, too career-oriented.

And now? Could Ty make her lose her mind over him again?

Sighing, she closed her eyes and shivered with pleasure as his strides ate up the distance to her bedroom.

This wasn't a time for thinking or analysing or remembering the past.

This was about here, now and the pleasure she knew only he could give.

As he laid her on the bed her eyes fluttered open and she gazed into the face of the sexiest man she'd ever known. He was all hers, even if it was only for a week.

'I'll be back. Wait for me.'

He feathered a kiss across her lips and she watched him walk out the door, transfixed by the perfection of his body.

Not that he had to ask. She wasn't going anywhere as long as he came back soon and doused the flames that were threatening to burn her alive. Stretching her arms overhead, she savoured the languorous heat that started at her toes, flowed to her fingertips and all the places in between, luxuriating in the feeling of being a desired woman.

'You're incredible.'

Gazing into her eyes, he lay down beside her, slowly running his hand down her arm, and she trembled beneath his touch and turned towards him, eager to feel him flush against her again.

'Uh-uh. Not so fast.'

He smiled, an intimate, sensual smile designed just for her, the type of smile she'd melted under countless times before as he stilled her frantic hands, capturing her wrists and holding them overhead. Reaching behind her neck, he freed the knot holding her bikini bra up and her breath hitched as the Lycra tumbled onto the bed, baring her breasts.

'Oh, Ty,' she murmured as he blew on her damp skin, the ferocity of his gaze burning her with its intensity. 'Please...'

'I know, sweetheart. I know.'

He nibbled at her mouth, her jaw-line and trailed lower, leaving a scorching line of fire branded against her skin and she caught her bottom lip between her teeth to keep from crying out.

He stilled for an instant, caressing her cheek with the tenderness she'd always found so surprising in a man of his profession, a man who relied on cunning and power and brute strength to obtain a mission objective.

'Is this what you want?'

Another typical Ty trait: honour. He was giving her an out, one she had no intention of taking him up on.

'Definitely.'

She nodded shyly and his cheeky grin sent her heart lurching for cover.

Her heart? Not good.

This had to be just sex. She couldn't risk anything more.

Physical, she could do.

Emotional, no way.

'What else would my boss like?'

He trailed his lips down her stomach, not waiting for an answer, every kiss teasing her, torturing her, making her want him more than she'd ever wanted anything in her life.

'Surprise me,' she murmured, though he didn't seem to hear, all his attention focussed on her body.

She should have been self-conscious as the afternoon sunlight streamed into her bedroom, but with Ty gazing at her body with reverence she felt like a goddess.

'Okay,' he murmured a second before his tongue hit her navel, laving it thoroughly as her hips arched off the bed and her desperate need for him went into orbit.

'So, that's a definite yes, then,' he murmured as he slid his hands under her butt and raised her towards him.

Feather-light kisses skimmed along her bikini line before he pressed his mouth against the wet material and she gasped as the heat of his mouth burned through the clinging Lycra, sending her one step closer to electrifying oblivion.

'Here. Let me.'

He tugged at the side strings, peeling the bikini bottoms away in one fluid motion before returning to exploring her intimate folds with his talented tongue.

Her mind and body took flight as he probed and suckled the swollen flesh of her core, sending her into another plane as she arched into his mouth, yelling his name.

Several mind-blowing, exquisite moments later she lay limp, barely aware as he shimmied up to lay alongside her once again.

Maybe her memories were foggy, maybe it had been too long since she'd had sex, but whatever the reason Ty had just sent her to heaven and back.

They'd always been good together but wow!

'We have lift-off,' he whispered against the side of her mouth, wearing a smile and little else as he draped an arm across her body.

'And how.'

Rousing herself out of her blissful stupor, she reached towards him, the sight of his erection sending shivers through her body all over again.

'When did those come off?' She pointed to the wet trunks lying in a sodden puddle on the floor.

'About the same time yours did—' Ty bit back the rest of his words as she took him in her hands.

'How about we swap roles for now? You're the boss and I'm the Odd Bod. Tell me what you want, Ty.'

She gently squeezed, sliding her hand up and down his shaft, remembering how much he liked foreplay as much as she did.

He groaned as his thumb caressed her nipple. 'You're doing just great on your own, sweetheart. No instruction from me needed.'

Tyler tensed as her fingers lightly brushed over the head of his straining penis, pleasure and pain warring as he barely held onto what little control he had left.

He'd waited for this moment since he'd first laid eyes on Kate again and having her satisfied and hot and horny in his arms was almost too good to be true.

'Sure?'

She wrapped her fingers around his length, moulding to it, blowing his mind, and he stilled her hand before he lost it completely.

'Hell, yeah.'

She'd just shattered whatever self-control he had with her tentative yet firm grip and he reached towards the bedside table, quickly ripping open the foil pack he'd had the sense to grab earlier, and sheathed himself.

'Glad someone's prepared,' she said as she watched him, the gold flecks in her eyes glowing fiery amber, the exact colour of the Sahara at dusk last time he'd been stationed there.

He lowered his weight back onto the mattress, his heart pounding at the need reflected in her beautiful face.

'Why did you think I went out before?'

She draped a long leg over his, tempting, hot, seductive. 'I didn't care as long as you came back.'

His heart clenched at the vulnerable look that flickered across her face and warning bells clanged in his head.

Maybe this wasn't such a great idea.

He didn't want to hurt Kate. What if she wanted more than he was willing to give, more than just this week?

He'd had his doubts about her ability to separate the past and the present but he'd doused whatever doubts he had with a good healthy dose of lust. Maybe he should've listened a little harder to his voice of reason, the same voice that had served him well through the hairiest of missions?

However, his conscience didn't stand a chance when she rubbed against him with her warm, slick entrance that led straight to heaven, sending his good intentions skyward too.

Knowing nothing could ever feel as good as this, he probed gently before sliding into her welcoming heat, the sheer rush of pleasure making him groan.

'Katie, you feel so good.'

She stared at him from beneath long eyelashes, desire blazing in her eyes, and the depth of her passion shocked him, that she should want him as much as he wanted her.

It was written in her eyes, in her face; she couldn't have spelled it out any clearer, and the thought that this beautiful, amazing woman wanted him was humbling beyond belief. He wouldn't disappoint her.

'You've been calling me Katie,' she whispered, something akin to awe spreading across her face as he started to rock.

'Do you like it?'

He increased the tempo, sliding out and thrusting into the hilt, encouraging her to join him on a wild and unrestrained ride.

Her answering moan fuelled his fire. 'I haven't heard it in a while. Only you've ever called me that. I like it.'

'Do you like this too?'

He couldn't wait any longer as her response took him to the next level, striving to give them both the ultimate pleasure, eager to give her the world if he could.

He hadn't thought she could climb any higher after her first shattering orgasm but he'd been wrong. Very wrong.

Her breasts swayed as he pounded into her and her short, panting cries urged him to the end, each powerful thrust bringing them closer to the edge, their voices blending as they tumbled over, clinging to each other.

Collapsing onto the bed, he exhaled slowly. If they'd burned up the sheets six years earlier it had nothing on the heat they generated now.

He'd lost his mind, shot to the stars and was still dazed as he realized that walking away from something this good, again, was going to be harder than any dangerous mission he'd ever had to face.

Silence enfolded them, broken only by the sound of ragged breathing as the realisation hit that this might've been more than just sex for him. Hell.

'Wow.'

She gave a low, husky laugh against his chest as she curled into him and he pushed aside his awkward thoughts and concentrated on Kate.

He snuggled her closer and grinned. 'If this is what being an Odd Bod's all about, shackle me for ever and throw away the key.'

'Be careful what you wish for…'

Her soft voice trailed off, hitting him where he was most vulnerable.

His conscience.

Kate might've said she wanted nothing from him beyond this week, but in the past she'd wanted to play for keeps.

Then what the hell was she doing playing with him now?

'What a dummy.'

Kate stepped out of the shower, aching in places she hadn't ached for a long time, though pleasantly so. The afternoon had been incredible and if the number of torn foil packets in her bin was any indication she would be aching for a while yet.

However, that wasn't the reason she was chastising herself as she towelled dry. The sex had been amazing, it was the aftermath that had her cringing. She'd been stupid enough to snuggle up to Ty, chatting about the years since she'd last seen him and expecting to have a light supper in bed before resuming where they had left off that afternoon.

Wrong. He'd barely lasted thirty minutes, holding her as if she were a ticking time bomb before beating a hasty retreat with a mumbled excuse about meeting someone.

So much for post-coital bliss.

She slipped into a sweatshirt and track pants and padded into the kitchen, needing comfort food. Ice cream or chocolate would do. At this point, anything with sugar in it would pass. Grabbing a pack of choc-chip cookies, she flopped into a nearby chair and tore the top off.

Who had she been trying to kid, convincing herself that one week with him would be enough? The afternoon's horizontal activities had well and truly put paid to that brilliant idea.

One taste and she was hooked all over again.

Being addicted to Ty was way too dangerous and she'd been stupid enough to kick-start the habit.

A knock on the front door roused her and she padded into the hallway to open it.

'Surprise. Thought I'd drop by with that material you were after.'

Though Di smiled at her, Kate watched her PA's gaze wander past her shoulder and into the room behind. No prizes for guessing who she was trying to catch a glimpse of.

Kate opened the door further. 'Come on in.'

Di winked. 'Only if I'm not interrupting anything.'

'You're not.'

'That's not what it looks like to me.' Di wiggled her eyebrows suggestively.

'Huh?'

Kate wondered if she was that easy to read. Surely the fact that she'd just had the best sex of her life didn't show?

'You've got that look, boss.'

Di handed over a pile of work, sat on the couch and folded her legs under her, her cheeky smirk saying it all.

'What look? Want a drink?'

Kate shook her head, hoping her hair would hide the guilty smile that was getting harder to disguise by the minute.

Di waggled her index finger. 'Don't distract me with beverages. I came here for gossip, not coffee. And that look says you've been swimming with the SEALs.'

Heat seeped into Kate's cheeks at the memory of what her afternoon dip with Ty had led to.

'So? What's the harm in that?'

Di ran a hand through her blonde spikes, re-creating her trademark porcupine look with little effort. 'I knew it! You got wet and wild with that guy. Details, I want details.'

'Not much to tell. We're getting along okay.'

Kate shrugged, determined to play down her involvement with Ty.

'What aren't you telling me?'

'Nothing.' Kate's mutinous silence didn't deter Di.

Her assistant hugged her knees and leaned forward, as if she had all the time in the world to listen. 'Spill it.'

What could she say? That she was falling for her ex all over again? How stupid would that be considering he'd made it clear he'd be out of her life again in a few days?

'I don't get it. Looks like you two have hit it off. Why don't you just enjoy the week with Adonis and who cares what happens after that?'

That was just it. Kate *did* care.

She cared a lot and it scared her. And if there was one thing she didn't do it was scare easy.

She'd survived a rough childhood with a bitter mother who blamed her for her father's absence.

She'd survived a new start in a strange country and she'd forged a fabulous career.

She was an Aussie battler and never stayed down for long.

So what was she doing wishing her week of having fun would turn into something more?

Di's squeal broke Kate's silence.

'Oh, no. You've fallen for him, haven't you?' She smacked her head. 'Girlfriend, what are you thinking?'

Kate smiled at Di's theatrics. 'I wasn't.'

'The idea of buying a man is to use him, not the other way round. See what happens when you don't get out much?'

'I get out enough.'

Kate knew that falling for Ty again had nothing to do with the number of men she had or hadn't dated. The minute she'd seen him at the auction she'd wanted him all for herself, past or not. 'Can we change the subject, please?'

'Whatever. Though you call me if you need me, okay? I have to get back to the office. How did you wangle a week to work from home anyway? I thought Henry had you under serious pressure?'

'Henry's not that bad. He knows I'm a professional. I'll deliver the story he wants whether I'm in the office or not.'

She wished she could tell Di about the promotion but she couldn't. Henry would announce his retirement and replacement in his own good time.

Di cast her a strange look. 'If this is what having a man around does to you, perhaps you should go back to being single.' She stopped at the doorway and looked Kate up and down. 'And a word of advice. Lose the sweats. Maybe that's why you're not getting any.'

'I'm getting plenty!' The words flew out of Kate's mouth before she could think.

Di poked her head around the closing door. 'Gotcha. Knew I'd get details out of you eventually. See ya round, chickadee.'

Kate poked her tongue out at Di's retreating back.

So much for not thinking about Ty. Chatting with Di had cemented the thoughts that had been whirling around in her head since he'd left and unfortunately, once acknowledged, the facts couldn't be ignored.

She was falling for him. Again.

And there wasn't one damn thing she could do about it.

CHAPTER NINE

TYLER had never run away from anything in his life. Even as a kid he'd stood his ground and fought his own battles and since joining the Navy standing up for what he believed had become ingrained, entrenched, and unshakeable. It was part and parcel of being a SEAL.

Then why had he run out of Kate's house as if the enemy were on his tail? To make matters worse he'd acted like a complete jerk in the process.

Retreat had been his only defence when he'd held her in his arms and listened to her anecdotes. If he hadn't run he would still be cocooned in her bed, enjoying the feeling of belonging there way too much.

He couldn't do it.

Why build false hope when all they had together was a week?

At least they had that and making love with Kate had blown his mind. She'd been insatiable, matching his needs in every way, as if she remembered all his erogenous zones and all the ways to please him.

Damn it, after a week with her he'd never be the same again. She'd raised the bar in more ways than one.

And what had he done? He'd run.

He could've cradled her in his arms all evening but the minute she'd started talking to him like the good old days he'd bolted.

He needed time out. No use letting their intense attraction get in the way of logic and no matter how Kate made him feel or how much he wished things could be different, they weren't. He'd made a promise to himself and he'd stick to it. He'd just have to stay focussed on the mission at hand—which was to enjoy every precious second with Kate—and not think beyond this week.

Strolling into the rec room at the base, he headed for the corner table where Bear sat nursing a giant coffee. The big guy's call on his cell phone had been welcome. His friend had mentioned something about saving the orphanage and he'd been hooked. Though in fairness Bear could've talked about walking on water and he would've been hooked, anything to wrench his thoughts away from Kate and how she made him feel.

'Howdy, Bear. What's happening?'

Bear shook his hand and kicked out the chair opposite. 'Could ask you the same thing. How's the odd-job business going?'

Tyler helped himself to coffee from a nearby machine and sat down. 'Remember that mission to Liberia? Way easier.'

Bear let out a long, low whistle. 'That bad, huh?'

'Worse.'

'This woman's got your number, huh?'

'Oh, yeah. And she knows just how to punch all the right buttons.'

Bear chuckled. 'Never thought I'd see the day, TJ taken down by a woman. Good one.'

No, it wasn't good. Not by a long shot. The more time he spent with Kate, the harder it would be to walk away. He'd already done it once and it had almost killed him.

This time it would be damn near impossible: he liked being in her cosy house, in sharing simple things like dinner, a swim, a bathroom.

He liked the feeling of belonging, of cohabiting with her, of feeling her gaze on him.

Hell, he liked it all and he was going to pay for it the minute he walked out of her life and the old terror gripped him: the loneliness, the urge to call her and the fear that he'd weaken and wouldn't be able to follow through on his promise to put her needs first whatever the cost to himself.

He'd thought he had a handle on loneliness as a kid, hiding behind a nonchalant façade, acting tough, and the persona had served him well enough as he'd existed within four walls of equally tough kids who'd also turned against the world and all its injustice. He'd survived alone and learned a valuable lesson along the way. Never depend on anyone. Ever. He relied on number one: no disappointment, no expectations, no pain, just the way he liked it.

He'd just have to remind himself of that the next time Kate looked at him with those hazel eyes of hers, drawing him in deeper and swifter than quicksand.

One thing was for sure—handling loneliness as a kid would be easy compared with what he'd have to face losing her this time around.

'What did you want to talk about, Bear?'

'Just wanted to chew the fat over a couple of ideas to save the orphanage. I was wondering if Team Eight could do anything. A marathon? Triathalon? You know the guys. They're always up for a challenge.'

'Thanks for the offer but I'm working on it.'

'How so?'

'I've persuaded Kate into doing some publicity by placing a big article in her magazine.'

Bear grinned. 'I'm not going to even ask what methods you used to *persuade* the lady in question.'

'Can it. I got enough grief the other night from Jack. I don't need it from you too.'

His friend seemed to sense his mood. 'This isn't serious, is it?'

'Depends on your interpretation of serious.' Tyler paused and stared into his coffee, knowing he had to confide in someone before he bust a gut. 'We were engaged once. How's that for serious?'

His friend's jaw dropped. 'What?'

Tyler nodded and managed a wry grin. 'Yeah, told you. Real serious.'

'What the—?'

'We met six years ago. She'd just come over from Australia, I'd just completed BUD/S training. We both kinda lost it for a while there.'

'You, engaged?' Bear shook his head, a stunned expression on his weather-worn face.

'It was a bit of a lark, really. She proposed to me, I jokingly said yeah, but we never got round to making any plans. We were both starting out on our careers; it wouldn't have made sense to stay tied. Not with me traipsing the world on missions never sure if I'd return or not. Anyway, it's all ancient history now.'

History. As in *the past*.

He'd be a damn sight better off if he remembered it.

What they shared now had to be a logical extension of two people who'd once hooked up for all the wrong reasons getting reacquainted. Nothing more. It couldn't be.

Bear opened and closed his mouth several times before managing to speak. '*Engaged*? No way. You never said anything. Does anyone know?'

'No. And I'd like to keep it that way. Besides, we only lived together for a few months. We were practically kids. It's no big deal.'

His friend swiped a hand over his face as if waking from a long sleep. 'Okay, you two were once an item, now you're trailing after her for a week? You gonna explain or what?'

Tyler shrugged. 'Nothing to explain. We've been apart for six years, she turned up at the auction and bought me, we're spending a week together and that's that. End of story. No complications, just two people catching up.'

When he put it like that it sounded so simple, so logical. Then why did his heart feel as if it had been twisted and ripped in half?

Bear paused, downed the last of his coffee and cast a puzzled look his way. 'Why are you still running, TJ?'

Tyler hated when his best friend was right. They'd been dive buddies for a long time before his knee blew out and Bear knew him better than anyone.

'I'm not. I just like to move around.'

'Yeah, I've heard that one before. You've been running your whole life and looks like nothing has changed. Have you told her about the physical?'

'What for?' Tyler glared, annoyed by his friend's accurate assumptions and wishing Bear weren't spot on. 'It's not relevant.'

Besides, he didn't want Kate's pity if he didn't pass and had to leave his beloved Navy behind, nor did he want her sticking around, maybe spending more time with him out of some warped sense of loyalty for what they'd once shared.

She deserved better. He'd always felt that way, which had made walking away the first time around just about bearable. He just had to remember it at the end of this week too.

Bear shook his head. 'If I need to tell you that you're wrong you're dumber than you look. You better do some thinking, man, and quick. Starting now.'

'What's there to think about? Kate's a great girl. She's intelligent, gorgeous and on her way to the top. What would she want with a washed-up SEAL who has no idea what to do with his life?'

There, he'd voiced his inner thoughts out loud, the same thoughts that had driven him out of her house when he'd realised that making love with her had been more about re-establishing emotional links with someone he still cared deeply about rather than a simple physical release.

Bear folded his arms and leaned forward, fixing him with the intimidating glare that had caused many a recruit to take a backward step.

'You're full of trash. In all the time I've known you I've never seen you spend more than a few dates with one woman, let alone get engaged to any of them. Now here you are giving me some spiel about how this wonder-woman is too good for you? Come on, TJ. I know you better than that. You've still got a thing for her and you're running scared, just like I said before.'

His friend stood and shrugged into his bomber jacket, shaking his head. 'Jeez, you've got it bad. I'll be damned. Anyway, I have to report in to the Chief. Later.'

Tyler watched his friend exit the bar and breathed a sigh of relief. If he'd wanted an interrogation he'd have allowed himself to be captured years ago. Bear was no slouch and had him pegged.

He *had* spent a lifetime running away from his demons.

How ironic that it looked as if the past might catch up with him yet?

Kate stretched, rubbed her eyes and looked at the clock in amazement. She never slept as late as nine.

Must've been all the exercise yesterday.

She ignored the thought and pushed out of bed, taking a full minute to realise that Ty wasn't around.

He hadn't returned last night.

So much for getting reacquainted. He'd had one taste and run ten miles in the opposite direction.

Swiping a hand across her gritty eyes and silently cursing herself for being such a fool, she stuck her feet into faded floral flip-flops and padded into the kitchen. Switching on the percolator, she leaned against the benchtop, surprised when the doorbell rang.

Hating the way her pulse quickened at the hope it could be Ty, she opened the door, her traitorous heart lurching at the sight of her errant houseguest wearing tight black jeans and matching T-shirt, a hint of dark stubble covering his jaw. The ultimate bad boy in the flesh; and she was so tired of being good.

'Brought you breakfast.'

He held out a bag of muffins with a slight smile playing about his mouth. That oh-so-gorgeous mouth with lips that had tasted and teased and driven her insane with need yesterday.

'Peace-offering, huh?'

Opening the door wider, she took the bag, opened it and inhaled deeply; apple cinnamon, her favourite—and she was touched that he'd remembered while trying desperately not to show it.

He strolled into the living room as if he belonged there, looking way too relaxed while she stood there feeling like yesterday's news, something he'd read and discarded.

'Didn't know I needed one. Are you angry about something?'

She squirmed under his disconcerting stare. 'Not really. Though you didn't come home last night…'

She trailed off, mentally kicking herself for sounding like a nagging girlfriend. He might be her odd-job guy for a week but he owed her nothing.

'I had some stuff to take care of back at the base, so I crashed there. No big deal, right?'

'Right.'

She stomped into the kitchen, eager to put as much distance between them as humanly possible before she did something stupid like give him a welcome-home kiss. Or hit him for summing up what she already knew but didn't want to hear.

He was right, this wasn't a big deal and she had no right to question him about his whereabouts no matter how much it burned her up inside.

She busied herself with breakfast, ignoring his stare boring into her back as he followed her into the kitchen.

'Going for a run?'

She whirled around to find him lounging in the doorway, looking her up and down.

'No. I slept in these.'

It wasn't as if she had to impress anyone, least of all him.

He smirked. It should've dented his good looks yet predictably it didn't.

'Who made you the pyjama police anyway?'

She tossed her hair in an 'I don't give a damn what you think' action and bit into a muffin, savouring the burst of tart fruit and sweet spice, barely managing to swallow the first bite as he stalked towards her, a dangerous gleam in his eyes.

'Pull over, driver, and show me your licence.'

He placed his arms either side of her, effectively pinning her into a corner between the benchtop and the pantry, his lowered, husky voice rippling over her in a caress.

She shouldn't play this game. Didn't she have any self-respect?

What they'd shared yesterday hadn't meant a thing to him otherwise he would've stuck around, maybe for an all-night encore. Instead, she'd slept alone. Correction, she'd lain awake half the night alone, listening out for his return, hating herself for feeling so needy.

For her, making love hadn't just been about having fun, and now that she knew it she'd be a fool to go there again.

'Licence, driver?'

Desire flooded her body as he leaned towards her and a waft of fresh citrus soap hit her reeling senses, leaving her confused and dazed and yearning.

How could any red-blooded woman resist a sexy male at his teasing best?

'Uh…I don't have it on me,' she said, transfixed by the dark silver flecks in the blue sea of his eyes, captured by the unadulterated lust she glimpsed there.

He lowered his head one infinitely slow inch at a time till his lips brushed hers in a barely there kiss.

'Then I'll just have to frisk you,' he whispered against the corner of her mouth, her heart flipping in sync with her common sense.

Screw common sense.

She'd done the sensible thing her whole life, particularly since Ty had walked out of it. She'd been the epitome of a good little career girl striving straight for the top and where had it got her? Successful in the boardroom, barely a ripple in the bedroom.

In some warped way maybe this was a golden opportunity to show Ty that cosying up to him in bed yesterday hadn't been a sign that she cared, that she could do the casual thing and stay emotionally detached.

If anything, she needed to prove it to herself. She might have fallen for him again but that didn't mean she had to lose the plot completely.

They'd always set the world on fire physically. Why not prove that making love didn't have to involve complication of feelings? Yeah, there was only one way to prove it and that was lose herself in Ty again.

Happy with her self-rationalisation—even if a small part of her recognised that her logic was flawed—she moulded her lips to his, opening her mouth under his increasing pressure.

Their tongues tentatively met, reaching to explore further as heat flooded through her. He nibbled on her bottom lip, sucking gently before dipping his tongue into her mouth once again, teasing her, pleasing her.

Flawed logic? What logic?

The minute his lips had touched hers again she'd been a goner. Wasting precious seconds rationalising anything when it came to this guy was foolhardy.

She was putty in his hands; always had been, always would be.

'So, are you going to arrest me?' she managed to say as his lips trailed towards her ear lobe, planting delicate butterfly kisses along the way and making her melt into a puddle of need.

'Still hung up on being bound to me, huh?'

He licked the delicate skin behind her ear, sending sparks shooting along every nerve-ending in her over-sensitised body as she arched towards him, desperate for more, desperate for him to assuage the growing tension winding her body tighter than a spring.

'Whatever turns you on.' She gasped as he finally reached for her and pulled her flush against him, her body tingling all over at the contact, the remaining muffin clutched in her hand pulverised into crumbs and scattering on the floor like the last remnants of her resistance.

She reached for him blindly, sliding her hands underneath his T-shirt, her fingertips tracing a light path down the warm skin, encouraged by his swift intake of breath.

'Does this turn you on?'

He ground his hips in a slow, undulating rhythm, leaving her breathless and dizzy with need.

'Or maybe this?'

He slid his hands under her top, cupping her breasts as fire streaked from his erotic touch to the very heart of her.

'Or this?'

He trailed a hand across her stomach and lower, much lower…

'I want it all,' she ground out, wondering where all reason fled to when Ty touched her.

She'd always been like this around him: yearning, melting, hungry for him, and it looked as if nothing had changed. Right now she was ravenous and staring in wonder at a virtual smorgasbord of delicacies all wrapped up in one delectable, edible package.

'Greed is good,' Tyler murmured, his hands continuing their leisurely exploration of her body, every sweet curve a precious memory to be stored and savoured when he took the only option available and bailed on her at the end of this week.

Kate held onto him, unsteady on her feet, awakening every protective urge within him to hold her close and never let go.

'You've done something to my bones,' she said, her eyes glowing like polished topaz in the morning light streaming into the kitchen.

'And you've sure done something to mine.'

He leaned into her again to emphasise the point as she smiled, a self-satisfied grin that made him want to tease her for ever as she fiddled with his zipper.

'My, my. So I have.'

Her confident touch belied the feigned innocence on her face as he reached into his back pocket, thankful he'd had enough foresight to keep a condom in his wallet.

'Always prepared, huh?'

She reached for the foil packet, tore it and unrolled the latex over him in an instant. He'd never thought using protection could be erotic but Kate's skilled hands put paid to that preconception.

'Yeah, that's me. A regular Boy Scout.'

He stripped quickly, feasting his eyes on her exquisite body as she shimmied out of the baggy cotton, his erection giving a painful throb as he absorbed every gorgeous inch of her.

'Nothing boyish about you.'

The mischievous glimmer in her eyes as she stared at him

and opened her arms made him feel ten feet tall, as if he were the only man in the world for her.

But he wasn't. He couldn't be.

She needed a man to give her everything and he couldn't be that man no matter how much he wanted to.

Picking her up, he held her close, enjoying the sensation of her full breasts pressed against his chest, soft mounds against hard muscle.

'You make me feel so good.'

She stared directly into his eyes as her hips arched towards him, her legs wrapping around him, urging him on and he slid into her, filling every inch of her slick heat, groaning with the exquisite pleasure of it, watching her eyes widen as he moved within her. Slowly. Very slowly.

'The feeling's mutual, sweetheart.'

Withdrawing, he plunged into her again, the friction of his flesh inside her burning dampness sending him to the edge much faster than he wanted.

'This is so amazing,' she murmured, squeezing him tighter with her legs, egging him on with her low, soft moans, her panting answer spurring him on as he groaned and sank into her again and again, his thrusts reaching fever pitch.

Her ecstatic cries of release undid him completely and he exploded, the quick-fire spasms almost buckling his knees.

But not half as much as the mental detonation in his brain that signalled what he'd known since they'd made love yesterday: this was more than physical.

Hell.

He leaned his forehead against hers, hating how complicated things could get now that he'd finally acknowledged what he'd suspected all along, grasping at words that just wouldn't gel as she slanted her head and kissed him on the mouth.

'If that's a frisk, arrest me, please. With an extended non-parole period.'

'I wish I could, sweetheart. I wish I could.'

But there was no use wishing for the impossible and as he held her close he hoped she hadn't seen his bittersweet smile.

Kate tucked a strand of wayward hair behind her ear, put her glasses on and steadied her fingers over the keyboard.

'We've got to do this today. I have a deadline to meet.'

Ty sat across from her, leaning back in a chair with his hands clasped behind his head. The pose drew attention to his muscular chest, yet another distraction for her wandering thoughts. 'Guys don't make passes at girls who wear glasses, you know.'

She peered at him over the top of trendy rimless frames she'd spent a small fortune on. 'Didn't seem to stop you.'

He laughed, a rich, deep sound that rolled over her in comforting waves. 'Nothing could keep me away from you.'

'Even if you were Superman and I was kryptonite?'

He flexed his biceps, sending her hormones into overdrive again. 'I'd eat you for breakfast and fly you away into the wide blue yonder.'

She blushed, his words conjuring up visions of their morning in the kitchen. 'I think you've already done the first bit.'

His eyes glowed, an endless indigo ocean she could drown in. 'Yeah. And I'm already looking forward to lunch.'

She wrenched her attention back to the keyboard with great difficulty, her breathing coming in short, shallow bursts at the anticipation of what 'lunch' he had in mind.

'Stop it. I need to concentrate. Can we get started?'

She tried a glare on for size, sending him a warning glance she hoped spoke volumes. In reality, she felt like Bambi trying to stare down a tiger.

Thankfully, he got the message. 'Okay, okay. Fire away.'

'Why did you become an instructor?'

'An injury during active duty. Can't tell you the details, though. If I did, I'd have to kill you.'

He grinned and her heart turned over for the hundredth time since she'd first laid eyes on him again.

Yeah, he'd kill her all right, with a smile rather than a stake straight through her heart.

'Okay, funny boy. Why teach driving skills to recruits?'

'Because I've always liked using a vehicle as a means of escape or a weapon of survival. Whether the bad guys are attempting a car-jacking, a kidnapping or a terrorist assassination, our response is the same. Get out of the situation quickly. That's where the expertise in handling a vehicle comes in.'

Her fingers flew over the keys, typing as he spoke. She couldn't resist a peek at his face, noting pride etched into the lines of experience, hearing the enthusiasm in his voice. He loved his work and it showed.

'Do you have any other options as an instructor?'

'I can always quit my day job and concentrate on instructing you in the finer art of—'

'Ty! Just answer the question.' She stifled a giggle at the mock chastised look on his face.

'Sure, I've got plenty of choices. We've got pathfinder school, sniper school, hand-to-hand combat school. And that's just for starters.'

'Do you have any favourite areas of expertise apart from vehicle training?'

He moved the way he'd been trained, with stealth and deadly precision, and wrapped his arms around her from behind before she'd even looked up from the keyboard.

'Yeah, I'm an expert in this area.'

He nuzzled her neck, his lips brushing her skin with the gentlest of touches.

She closed her eyes for a moment and leaned back, relishing the feel of his strong arms holding her tight and wishing that he would never let go. However, that dream was futile and she knew it.

Besides, she had a story to write and a promotion to gain. Despite the pleasant distraction of Ty in her life she couldn't lose sight of her main goal. Being Chief Editor would sustain her in the years ahead, which was more than could be said for the heartbreakingly gorgeous SEAL who would walk out on her any day now.

She broke the embrace with reluctance. 'Okay, point taken. Now, can we get back to work?'

'Slave driver,' he mumbled, resuming his place on the chair opposite.

She instantly missed the warmth and security of his arms. 'And don't you forget it. I'm ordering you to answer my question.'

She smiled as he extended his arms and crossed them, then blinked genie-style.

'As you wish, boss.'

'Well?'

He paused, feigning indifference. 'What was the question again?'

She picked up the nearest cushion and flung it at him.

He caught it with little effort, his reflexes lightning-fast. 'Okay, okay. My other areas of expertise include underwater operations, combat diving and jungle warfare.'

'Are all those courses taught here in LA?'

'No. Some aspects, like hydrographic reconnaissance, underwater demolition and jungle stuff are taught in Puerto Rico.'

'Any chance of you teaching over there?'

She held her breath, suddenly desperate to hear his answer yet simultaneously wanting to place her hands over her ears and yell 'la-la-la' so she couldn't hear him.

Why did she care?

Once this week was over he could go wherever he liked, do whatever he liked, with whoever he liked, just as they'd agreed.

A relationship wasn't for a guy like Ty; he'd proved it last time around. Yet somehow in the last forty-eight hours she'd found herself fantasising just a little too often about what it would be like if she didn't push him out of her life at the end of the week, about what it would feel like to give him another chance.

Apart from her job and her grandparents the last six years had been pretty empty without him. Would it be so bad to let him into her life again?

'You like having me around that much, huh?'

Damn, he'd turned her innocuous question into what it really was—a personal quest for information.

She shrugged, playing coy and hoping he bought it.

'Maybe.'

'I kind of grow on you, don't I?'

'Yeah, like a fungus.'

She hoped her quick retort would hide what she'd been about to almost admit—that she *did* like having him around. A lot.

'And here I was, thinking you'd fallen under my spell again.'

'I wouldn't be stupid enough to do that. Not when you'll be out of here in a couple of days.'

Now that she'd said the words out loud all she had to do was believe them.

He nodded. 'Smart girl. That's why we're having so much fun. We both know exactly where things stand.'

A knifelike pain stabbed at her heart. Smart? More like dumb. Dumb, dumb, dumb.

What had she expected, for him to fall down on his knees and profess he'd never forgotten her and move in permanently after making love a few times?

'Any more questions?'

She shook her head, unable to speak for a moment.

'Good. In that case, care to play hookey for a while?'

Her pulse raced in anticipation at the playful tone in his voice.

'What did you have in mind? I really need to get this article finished.'

'Leave it. Let's go for a drive.'

Willing to do anything to prolong the pleasure of whatever precious time they had together, she threw her pen and notepad down, barely having time to find her keys and lock up before he grabbed her hand and led her outside.

'Where are we going?'

He brushed a kiss across her lips, sending her heart rate into arrest mode. 'Trust me.'

He didn't have to say the words. She did trust him, body and soul. Unfortunately, she also knew that blind trust could end up breaking her heart. Again.

CHAPTER TEN

TYLER didn't like questions.

He always felt as if he were being interrogated by the enemy and the damned thing was they always led to answers. Right now he didn't want to think or analyse. He just wanted to feel, to enjoy the company of his beautiful Kate for the little time they had left and not think about the consequences.

Kate's questions had been easy enough till she'd honed in on the future. He didn't want to think about it, let alone respond to questions he didn't know the answers to.

'This is some view,' he said, leaning both arms against the car roof and taking in the sweeping LA vista he'd come to appreciate in the short space of time he'd spent at her place.

She smiled, pride evident in her face, and it struck him how much she loved her home. 'Yeah, the house may not be up to the usual Beverly Hills mansion standard but the view is to die for.'

They stood in companionable silence as his gaze swept across the rolling hills dotted with cream-rendered movie-star homes, lush greenery and twinkling lights in the descending dusk. If he believed in fairy tales he could quite easily see himself coming home to this view, this house, this woman every day for the rest of his life.

But he'd given up on believing in happy endings a long

time ago and, no matter how much this whole scene tugged at his heartstrings, a guy had to do what a guy had to do.

Straightening, he turned to face her, only to find her staring at him rather than the sensational view.

'Hope you like Japanese food?'

He opened the car door for her and she slid onto the leather seat, her knee-length denim skirt offering him a tempting view of long, tanned legs and resurrecting memories of how they'd felt that morning wrapped around him.

'Love it.'

Gritting his teeth at the pain that ripped through his knee, he braced himself using his arms on the steering wheel before sliding in.

'Your knee giving you trouble?'

Waiting till the wave of nausea that washed over him at the excruciating burning in his knee subsided, he said, 'It's driving me nuts at the moment. Comes with the job, I guess.'

'You should see someone about it.'

'Uh-huh,' he mumbled, needing a change of topic and fast. 'You've only got a couple of days left to order me around. Anything special you want me to do for you?'

'How about nightly foot rubs, a manicure, a night out at the theatre and a five-course meal?'

Kate kept her voice light-hearted, determined to hide the hurt piercing her soul. She'd tried voicing her concern and he didn't want it.

Not that it surprised her. He didn't want her concern or anything else she had to offer beyond this week and though she'd made a conscious decision to live for the moment and walk away at the end, the practice was a lot harder than the theory and she was floundering badly.

If Ty found out she'd fallen for him he'd have a field-day. Or else bolt in the opposite direction before the week was out, leaving her heartbroken into the bargain.

'How about we start with a rub and see what follows from there?'

His low, seductive voice washed over her, warming her better than the car's heater as once again her common sense took a back seat to her treacherous body.

'I think we both have a fair idea.'

Despite her flippant response, she secretly liked the way his mind worked. If the only attention he paid her for their remaining time together was aimed below the belt, she'd take whatever she could get. 'So theatre is out?'

'I'm not great with the fancy stuff. If you need a penguin to take you out, you're playing with the wrong guy.'

'I'd rather have a SEAL.' She paused, biting back the next words but they popped out anyway. 'And who says I'm playing?'

An ominous silence hung between them and she wished he'd say something, anything, to bridge the awkwardness of the moment.

'Don't go getting serious on me, Kate. I'm not the guy for you. I don't play for keeps, as we've already established.'

He sounded more distant than ever, his gaze fixed on the road ahead.

If he'd called her sweetheart or Katie she might have been able to laugh it off. However, he didn't and the use of her proper name reinforced the seriousness behind his words. He meant every word and, boy, did it hurt.

'Yeah, I know. Why do you think I only bought you for a week? It's not like I want to give us a second chance or anything.'

Her laughter sounded forced and she swallowed, trying desperately not to cry. Thank goodness they were having this conversation in the car and he couldn't see her face.

Unfortunately he sensed her distress and pulled the car over to the side of the road at the Gucci end of Rodeo Drive and she nibbled on her bottom lip, keeping her gaze firmly fixed on the designer shops and constant parade of tourists rather than face the inevitable now that she'd been stupid enough to hint at the truth.

Ty grabbed her hand and she had no option but to turn to face him.

'Listen to me. You need a guy to be there for the long haul, a guy who's going to be around for ever. I'm not him. You need stability, someone to give you everything you deserve and more. You need something I can't give you.'

Holding back a sob, she murmured, 'So now you're trying to tell me what I need?'

She tried to pull her hand away but he squeezed tight.

'You're saying I'm wrong?'

She glared at him, tucking a wayward strand of hair behind her ear, her fingers shaking. 'I'm saying you don't know the first thing about me any more.'

He let her go, the sadness in his eyes leaving her bereft.

'Maybe you're right, but I know one thing. There is no future for us beyond this week. If you can handle that, we keep having fun for the next few days. If not, I walk now.'

Taking a steadying breath and trying to ignore the ache in the vicinity of her heart, she said, 'So that's what you're calling sex these days. Having fun?'

'Well, isn't it? What would you call it?'

She wanted to scream 'making love' but managed to hold her tongue. She'd made enough of a fool of herself for one night. She had all the answers. There was nothing left to say.

Lifting her chin and blinking back the sting of tears, she looked him straight in the eye.

'You're right. It's been fun. How about we have dinner and go ho—back to my place.'

If he noticed her slip up he didn't say. She couldn't bear the thought of using his name and 'home' in the same sentence, not ever again.

She would take what little he had to offer for the remainder of their time together, lock away her emotions and throw away the key. One thing she couldn't bear to live with was regret; she'd lived a lifetime of it already, wishing she'd reached out to him six years ago and told him how she'd really felt rather than pushing him away with her own ambition.

She wouldn't make the same mistake with him again. If all he could offer her was the next few days, she'd take it.

'If that's what you want.'

He restarted the engine after staring at her a moment longer.

I want it all.

She quashed the unbidden reply, knowing she'd never have it. At least not with Ty, the only man who mattered.

Tyler's plan had been an unmitigated disaster. He'd wanted to escape after playing twenty questions with Kate that afternoon.

So what had he done? Taken her to dinner only to have the conversation to end all conversations in the car on the way there. Ironic that it had occurred on Rodeo Drive, with its fancy boutiques and cafés, places Kate was probably familiar with, places as far away from his world as it was possible to get.

They were so different, destined to not be together despite the magnetic physical pull that kept him anchored to her side. As for the emotional bonds they'd reforged…he wouldn't go there.

He'd hurt her, no doubt about it. He'd seen the tears glistening in her eyes when he'd told her there was no future for them. Hell, it had taken every ounce of his self-control not to reach out to her, to tell her he'd like to hold her for ever.

For ever.

Nothing lasted that long and he wasn't about to take a huge risk in finding out if a relationship with Kate could change all that. No way.

She'd surprised him with her bravado all through dinner, making casual small talk as if her life depended on it. However, he hadn't been fooled. He'd seen the sadness in her eyes, the hurt behind her smile that he'd put there with his personal brand of God's honest truth. Honesty had served him well in the past. What the hell had gone wrong now?

He stared at the ceiling, hands clasped behind his head to stifle the impulse to punch his pillow. He knew exactly what had gone wrong. Honesty only worked if you faced the truth yourself and in this case he hadn't. He'd fed Kate all the right lines about not being good enough for her, about not being around for the long haul.

But he hadn't bought it. Not any of it.

Rather than face the truth he'd buried it under a pile of excuses. She'd basically offered him more than a week with her half-veiled hints at playing for keeps and what had he done? Hidden his feelings behind cocky words as usual. After all, a SEAL couldn't show vulnerability. It went against the grain.

A SEAL also kept his promises, yet the more time he spent with Kate the harder it was to focus on what he wanted.

Pity was, he had no idea what that was now.

A week ago it had been easy: get through his physical and if he couldn't, put his thinking cap on and figure out what the hell he wanted to do with his life.

He didn't do emotional entanglements for this very reason. Why let down someone else when he couldn't be the man he'd spent his life trying to be?

Kate deserved more.

She deserved a full, active life, to continue making leaps in her career, not to be bound to some surly tempered has-been with a bust knee. And he knew without a shadow of a doubt that if he couldn't be a SEAL in any capacity following his physical, he'd be a nightmare to be around.

Kate stirred and snuggled into him and he tensed.

With his thoughts a jumbled mess and guilt plaguing him at causing that defenceless look in her eyes, he hadn't laid a finger on her tonight. Instead, he'd cuddled her till she'd fallen into a restless sleep, ordering his libido to behave. Thankfully, it had worked.

Until now.

With her hands skimming his chest and her lips pressed against his neck, he was having a hard time of it. Very hard.

He tried to sidle away, disentangling her arms in the process.

'Ty, don't leave me.'

He stilled at her whispered plea and rolled towards her.

'Are you sure?' He gently kissed her forehead, wondering if she meant now or for ever.

Moonlight slanted through the window, bathing the room in a soft, silvery glow as her eyes glowed like a nocturnal cat in the reflected light, watching and waiting for his next move.

'Love me,' she whispered, her hands spreading over his chest and moving lower, effectively shattering his latent gallantry, which didn't want to make this situation any more complicated than it already was.

He might be a SEAL but he wasn't a saint, and with a muffled groan he pulled her on top of him, slanting his mouth across hers in a hungry kiss.

She shuddered as he parted her lips with his tongue, teasing her with tortured patience, grateful for the opportunity to obliterate his thoughts, to sate his unquenchable need for her, maybe for the last time.

Her lips were warm and soft, coaxing him into prolonging the pleasure. As she parted them and let him in, he kept the kiss slow…infinitely slower than he could have thought possible considering how she turned him on.

He'd always felt this way with her: ready and raring to go, unable to get enough of her, wanting her every minute of every day.

Walking away the first time had been hell and it looked as if he was headed on a one-way return visit.

However, she'd asked him to love her and that was what he intended on doing. All night.

He could give her that much at least.

'You're wearing too many clothes,' he said, playfully tugging at the oversized T-shirt she'd worn to bed, his fingertips skimming the smooth, velvety skin beneath and itching to fill his palms with it.

'So are you.'

She smiled, a coy, sexy upward turning of her kissable lips as she sat up, whipped the T-shirt over her head and threw it on the floor.

'Allow me.' She shimmied down his legs, taking his boxers with her. 'Better?'

His breath caught as her hair draped across his erection. He'd never seen anything so erotic and he burned the memory into his memory bank, knowing he'd never forget the incredible week they'd shared no matter what happened from here on in.

'Come here.' He crooked a finger at her.

'Hey, who said you could give the orders around here?' she murmured, a seductive glint in her eyes. 'Or is that an offer? Because I intend to. Over and over again.'

She flicked her tongue out over her lips and that one little gesture shot straight to his groin.

'That's it. You're in trouble.'

He pulled her down to the bed again and lay on top of her, the sensation of bare skin to skin notching up the heat sizzling between them an extra degree or two.

He'd been in some hot situations before while trapped under enemy fire or extracting civilians from war-torn countries, but nothing had his heart pounding or his body burning up on pure adrenalin as much as getting naked with Kate.

'Mmm…big trouble.'

She wriggled against his erection, driving all conscious thought from his brain.

'You make me crazy,' he said, rolling away for a second to protect himself before returning to one of his favourite positions and lowering his weight on top of her.

'And you make me horny,' she said, sliding her arms around him and raking her fingernails slowly down his back, her smile pure temptation.

'You've got a smart mouth.'

He nudged between her legs as her hips rose to meet him and slipped a finger into the moist curls between her thighs, rubbing softly till she whimpered.

'All the better to—'

He took her mouth, kissing her with all the passion in his soul, knowing that if this was as good as it got he'd die a happy man indeed.

'I love it when you talk dirty,' he murmured against the side of her mouth as she writhed beneath him, her wild, uninhibited cries ringing out before he brushed her lips again, their breath intermingling as she came in a loud scream of ecstasy.

Unable to hold back a second longer he sheathed himself quickly and pushed inside her silken, hot flesh, knowing that nothing came close to this indescribable feeling of being so warm, so tight, with her all around him.

His heart clenched as her eyes fluttered open, their luminous depths almost incandescent in the moonlight and her delicious mouth formed a small O as he started to move, sliding in and out, taking them to the brink.

As he thrust harder, deeper, her eyes widened and he could've sworn he could see right into her soul.

It finally hit him at the same moment as the force of his climax gripped him and sent him spiralling over the edge.

He loved her.

Enough to want to stay here like this, for ever.

But he couldn't do for ever so what now?

Looking down into her face, he pushed away the hair that

clung in tendrils to her heat-dampened skin, in total awe of the unique feeling that flooded every cell of his body and made him crave more.

Tell her.

Yeah, right. She'd think he was totally nuts. Driving her away this afternoon, saying he loved her tonight after mind-blowing sex?

Nah, the timing sucked. He'd have to do better than that. In fact, he needed to get his head around this startling revelation first before blabbing the first words that came into his mind.

Fortuitously, he didn't have a chance to say anything as Kate placed a finger against his lips.

'I know. We had fun. No words needed, James. That's an order.'

Tyler bit back a groan as she slipped out from under him and strolled into the bathroom, her butt glimmering like two perfect orbs in the moonlight.

Shaken to the core by the realisation he loved Katie, the woman he'd planned on walking away from once and for all shortly, he rolled onto his back and closed his eyes.

What the hell was he going to do now?

CHAPTER ELEVEN

As KATE typed the finishing touches to her story Ty strolled into the room and placed a mug next to her.

'Thought you might like a coffee.'

'Thanks.'

She clasped her hands behind her back and stretched, working out the kinks in her neck.

As Ty stared at her she quickly dropped her hands. By the intense look on his face he might take her stretching as an invitation to start massaging her neck again and that was one thing she couldn't cope with right now.

She had to focus her energy during the day to maintain a friendly camaraderie. She'd planned to keep the physical side of their relationship to nights, using the darkness as a shield to hide the emotion written all over her face whenever he touched her.

'Finished?'

He walked towards her, his long, tanned legs looking particularly delectable in running shorts. She noted the slight limp where he favoured his right leg and knew his knee was worse than he let on. He'd avoided talking about it and she hadn't pushed it.

So she had her head in the sand? Nothing new there. It just about summed up her whole attitude when it came to Ty.

Though that wasn't entirely true; he'd made it perfectly clear where she stood in their clear-the-air conversation in the car the other night and it still hadn't dimmed her pleasure in having him around. Go figure?

She sipped her coffee, trying to ignore the heat radiating off his legs as he stood beside her and looked over her shoulder.

'Yeah, all done. I'll drop it off later.' She shielded the laptop screen with a hand. 'And no peeking. If you want to see it, you'll just have to buy the magazine.'

He laid a hand on her shoulder, sending her pulse rate racing. 'Surely the star attraction of the article can take a look before it runs hot off the press?'

She shrugged his hand off, snapped the laptop shut and stood up. 'No. I've got to go.'

He smiled. 'You creative types are all the same. Touchy as hell when it comes to work. Why can't you e-mail it to your boss so we can spend our last day together?'

She shook her head, instantly quelling the irrational leap of joy at his suggestion. She wasn't that good an actress. Spending all day with him would just make it harder to act nonchalant.

Besides, they couldn't spend an hour in each other's company without ending up in the bedroom…or the kitchen… or the living room, without any clothes and having way too much fun. The more time they spent together, the more danger she was in of saying something else she would regret.

'Thanks for the offer but I want to run a few ideas past Henry for the orphanage article so I thought I'd drop by the office. See you later.'

She slung her bag over her shoulder, picked up her keys and walked out the door, trying to ignore the bemused expression on his face and barely acknowledging his wave.

Yeah, the office was the place to be right now, a perfect SEAL-free sanctuary.

However, if she'd thought that she could totally avoid him at the office, she was wrong. Di pounced as soon as she walked in.

'Managed to come up for air, huh?'

Kate wasn't in the mood for banter, though she couldn't fault her PA's inquisitiveness. She did the same thing whenever Di had a new man in her life, which seemed to be every few weeks. In fact, she'd lived vicariously through Di's tales a lot lately and it was nice to be on the receiving end for once.

Kate wiped her brow and flicked away imaginary perspiration. 'Yeah, though it's tough keeping up with a SEAL. All that training, you know. Gives them incredible stamina.'

Di's eyes widened and she leaned closer. 'Ooh, tell me more.' She paused, before placing her hands over her ears. 'On second thoughts, I don't want to hear. I'm jealous as hell. It's no fun when my old boss is getting some and I'm not.'

Kate patted her on the head, her hand not making a dent in the gelled blonde spikes. 'Tough luck. Some guys just go for the more experienced type.'

Di perked up at this. 'Hey! If it's experience he's after, I'm—'

'Too busy meeting deadlines to think about anything else. Now get back to work.'

Di saluted. 'Yes, boss,' and goose-stepped her way into the copying room.

Kate smiled and knocked on Henry's door, which opened in record time and Henry ushered her in. 'How's my replacement today? Got anything to show me?'

She couldn't believe it. Not only had her boss opened the door but he was smiling at her. Usually, he barked an instruction to enter from behind his desk and frowned through the whole interrogation, for that was what it was whenever anyone was summoned to his office, a succession of sharp questions that left you feeling as if you had faced a firing squad. He must be getting mellow as he neared retirement. Amen to that.

She handed him a printed copy of the article. Though she'd already e-mailed it to him, she knew he liked reading hard copies.

'All done. I'm also doing another piece to tie in with this one for the next issue.'

She took a steadying breath as Ty's image popped into her head, driving his deal home so she would run the story on the orphanage. 'The man auction was to raise money for the Ramirez Orphanage. However, it wasn't enough. The SEAL in this story believes that raising the profile of the orphanage will ultimately save it. I happen to agree.'

Henry speed-read the article she'd handed him. 'This is good stuff, Kate.'

He scratched his balding head for a moment. 'You've got yourself a promotion, girly. I'll announce you're my successor at the next staff meeting.'

He shoved the article on top of a pile of paperwork in his in-tray, signalling the end of the interview.

'About the other article?'

He waved her away. 'Since when have you needed my opinion on a story? If it's good enough for you, it's good enough for me. Now get back to work…Chief.'

Kate smiled and thanked him, desperately trying to keep her legs steady as she walked out of his office.

She'd done it. The dream job was hers and she couldn't wait to take up the position. Throwing herself into a new job would be the only way to distract herself from the heartache of losing Ty.

By the way her heart clenched and splintered at the thought of losing him, she was going to need all the help she could get.

Kate had to tell him.

Now that she had the job for sure there was no way she could keep it from Ty. He deserved to know. In fact, she should've told him earlier in the week or perhaps yesterday when she'd been grilling him.

But she'd been scared. Terrified of losing what little time they had left, petrified he'd accuse her of using him right from the start. And now that her feelings had developed into something deeper…

She had no other option but to come clean and pray to God the guy who valued honour above all else would understand where she'd been coming from.

Taking a deep breath, she unlocked the front door and stepped inside, the sight of her walking-talking fantasy leaning against the kitchen doorframe wearing cargo shorts, a sky-blue T-shirt that matched his eyes and a smile doing little for her false bravado.

'Hey there, gorgeous.'

'You talking to me?' she said, forcing a smile as she closed the door and crossed the room to drop a quick peck on his cheek.

His eyes widened in surprise but he didn't flinch; must be used to subterfuge attacks.

She'd never done anything like that before, but right now she desperately needed to be near to him, needed the physical reassurance he wouldn't run out the door as soon as she told him the truth.

'I don't see any other gorgeous, sexy females in the vicinity. Not that I'd see them with you around anyway.'

'Always the charmer,' she said, kicking off her stilettos and flopping down into the nearest chair, pointing to the sofa opposite. 'Want to take a seat? I need to talk to you about something.'

His smile faded as he sat, a slight furrow creasing his brow. 'Sounds serious.'

'Not really, but it's something I should've told you a few days ago if I wasn't such a chicken.'

Tension etched into every muscle of his body as he leaned back and rested an ankle on his good knee. 'Okay, what's up?'

She swallowed, trying to dislodge the lump of foreboding wedged in her throat. 'You know the article I just handed in? And why I really needed your input? Well, my boss pretty much blackmailed me into doing it in exchange for a huge promotion to Chief Editor. It's something I've wanted for ages and I've worked incredibly hard to get it.'

'And?'

Thankfully, he didn't appear annoyed. In fact, his shoulders had relaxed and he rested an arm across the back of the sofa.

'I didn't want you thinking I used you. You know, your co-operation with the story to get me where I wanted to go.'

He smiled, his bronze tan making his eyes glow an electrifying blue.

'So you used me? Must say, I kinda like your techniques at coercion.'

'You're not mad?'

He shook his head, a slight frown creasing his brow. 'Not unless you tell me that all this week has been about is securing that job for you.'

'No,' she murmured, pain clutching her heart and squeezing till she could barely breathe. Their week together had been so much more than that but she couldn't tell him. He didn't want to hear it. 'I think you know me better than that.'

'I do.'

He stood up, crossed the room and dropped down on his good knee next to her chair, taking hold of her hand and smiling up at her. 'See? It's not that serious. You got a promotion out of the story; we had a great week together. So relax.'

Easy for him to say.

He didn't have a giant lump lodged in his throat at the thought of their week ending right now, considering seven days had passed.

'It was pretty great, wasn't it?' she murmured, squeezing his hand, wishing she could convey half of what she was feeling through a simple touch.

'You bet.'

Leaning forward, he brushed a soft, lingering kiss across her lips and she sighed at the all-too-brief contact. 'I have to get back to the base. My CO called.'

'Oh, okay.'

She nodded, ignoring the sting of tears at the backs of her eyes, wishing he'd stop staring at her as if he didn't want to leave.

Maybe she should give it one last go? Tell him how she really felt?

'You're incredible, Katie, and I'll never forget you, but I've got to hit the road. You know how it is.'

Before she could respond he stood up, grimaced as he straightened his knee and headed for the spare room, leaving her on the verge of begging him to stay.

The sad thing was, she did know how it was. She'd sat back and watched him walk away once before, and if the pain had been devastating back then it was near on unbearable now.

Damn, she'd made a mess of this. She needed to convince him to stay, to give them longer than seven days, to take a chance at something potentially wonderful.

However, before she could form the words he was back, bag in hand, a stoic expression on his handsome face.

'Well, it looks like it's time for this sailor to ship out.'

He sent her a sharp salute and she forced a smile as she crossed the room to stand in front of him.

'What would you say if I asked you not to go?'

The murmured question hung between them for what seemed like an eternity as she stifled the urge to wrap her arms around him and bury her face in his chest when she glimpsed the sadness in his eyes.

'I'd say that's a big ask.' He shook his head. 'I'm sorry. I can't give you what you want.'

You can, she wanted to scream. She wanted to yell and rant and thump his chest for not seeing what was staring him right in the face.

She loved him. She needed him.

And it still wasn't enough.

She bit her lip, struggling to hold back tears as he stared at her with regret in his eyes. He'd read her mind other times; she just prayed he did it now.

'Take care, sweetheart.'

Her heart shattered as he picked up his bag and opened the door.

'Ty, I—'

'Don't make this harder than it already is,' he murmured as he stepped through the door and closed it without looking back.

She sank to the floor and cried, once more than she had in the last six years.

So much for the coping strategies she'd learned from the counsellor after her grandparents' death. She'd just flunked 'Getting a Grip 101' all over again.

Tyler screeched into the car park of the orphanage, gravel flying in his wake. He'd focussed all his attention on the road; driving through congested LA traffic when the roads were rain-slicked was hazardous at the best of times, but in his current frame of mind it could become lethal.

Though he felt like ramming something he didn't have a death wish. Besides, he couldn't kill what was already dead inside and that was exactly how he'd felt ever since leaving Kate's place.

Now, with the engine switched off and nothing left to focus on, the pain flooded back.

How could he have let this happen? Loving her, growing

attached to her, wasn't supposed to happen. He couldn't have ties, couldn't do it to her, yet when she'd asked him to stay he'd almost lost it and agreed.

He'd needed to get away ASAP and couldn't have retreated any faster. Their week was done. They were done. Now all he had to do was put it behind him.

Thumping the steering wheel in frustration, he glanced around, needing to focus on anything but the empty ache in his heart.

This place had been home for so long, since his foster parents had dropped him off one afternoon promising they would return. Almost thirty years later, he was still waiting.

He'd never figured out why two seemingly normal people could adopt a baby, only to dump him a few years later like unwanted baggage.

Until he'd blown his knee. It had all become crystal-clear then; the doc had said in all likelihood he had some kind of arthritis that was probably inherited and he might have displayed some signs as a child. After hearing that it didn't take a genius to figure out that first his mother, then his foster parents had ditched the crippled kid.

It was hard enough battling the increasing pain on a daily basis, but when he'd been with Kate he'd almost felt human again.

She'd crept under his guard and into his heart when he'd been determined to hold his emotions in check. He'd kept telling himself it was just about the sex till she'd opened her arms and welcomed him into her life, her house and he'd fallen head first into an emotional entanglement it would take a lifetime to recover from.

Someone tapped on his window and he looked up, the bleakness in his soul engulfing him till he wanted to thump something in frustration.

'Hey. Are you coming in? The kettle's on.'

He managed a smile for Mary. She'd always sensed when he was down and believed that a cup of tea was the elixir to happiness. He had a feeling it would take a hell of a lot more to cheer him up this time.

Taking a few calming deep breaths, he stepped from the car and she squeezed his arm. 'I've seen the kids look happier after vaccine shots. What's up?'

'I don't want to talk about it.'

He waved to a group of nearby children as they headed inside, something akin to pleasure warming his heart as they smiled back, the innocence lighting up their faces. It was a good sign if his heart could still feel emotion other than the ache enveloping it.

'You and Kate have a lovers' tiff?'

He looked down in amazement. 'How did you know we were lovers?'

She rolled her eyes. 'The air between you almost crackled that day you were here. Besides, I could tell by the way she looked at you. She's crazy about you.'

He watched Mary making tea. She would make someone a great wife one day and he hoped that her life outside the orphanage would start sooner rather than later. He owed it to her, just as he'd promised. If the orphanage could survive this time he would find someone else to run it so Mary could be free to lead her own life.

Yet another promise he needed to make good on.

Suddenly, a terrible thought flashed through his mind. What if Kate didn't run the article on the orphanage? He'd lived up to his side of the bargain and she'd secured her promotion because of it. Would she follow through on her side of the deal now that he'd shunned her request to stay and walked away?

'What did I say?' Mary pinned him with a concerned stare.

She fussed over him like a mother hen, always had, probably always would. He'd pretended he didn't like it as a kid when secretly he'd loved the attention. Most of the other orphans had been jealous but he hadn't cared. Mary as his big sister was just fine by him.

'She is, you know. Absolutely mad over you.'

'Hmm.'

He sipped the tea, scalding his mouth in the process. It just wasn't his day.

'Don't blow this. She could be the best thing that's ever happened to you.'

'Or the worst,' he mumbled into his cup, wishing that he could throw himself back into action in some war-torn country.

At least he'd known where he stood under threat from the enemy. Now, he had no artillery against the assault of an unforgettable woman who had crawled under his defences and led him to the brink of destruction.

Mary shrugged. 'I hope you know what you're doing.'

He didn't justify her response with an answer. Instead, they finished their tea in companionable silence before he brought up the safer topic of the children.

For an hour or so, Mary regaled him with tales of the kids' exploits, making him forget his own problems. It wasn't till later, after he'd said goodbye to Mary and the kids and walked to his car, that the problems resurfaced when he looked up to find Kate strolling straight towards him.

CHAPTER TWELVE

'HEY, Ty.'

Kate stared at him, those hazel eyes playing havoc with his mind while the rest of her had a field-day with other parts of his body.

He gritted his teeth against his first instinct to wrap her in his arms and never let go.

'What are you doing here?'

She'd changed into a red vest-top and faded denim jeans, both items fitting her body like a second skin, and he thrust his hands into his pockets to stop them from reaching out to touch her.

Her cool glance gave away nothing. If she could sense his discomfort, she wasn't showing it. 'I came to see Mary. I needed to clarify a few details before I write the article on this place.'

'So, you're going to do the article? That's great.'

She sent him a confused look. 'I said I would. Why would you think otherwise?'

He shrugged, knowing he was making a mess of this, but in a way maybe getting her mad at him would make walking away easier?

'I thought you might be angry about me refusing your offer to stay.'

She flushed, a slow blush that crept up her neck into her face and doing little to detract from her beauty.

'I'm not that petty,' she said, the gold flecks in her eyes glinting in the waning sunlight. 'Besides, I must've been crazy asking you to stay when I know you're the king of running away.'

'What's that supposed to mean?'

Surprised she'd partially guessed the truth, he wanted to know more even though she had no idea why he'd spent his life running away and was judging him for it.

'Come on, you ran away six years ago and you're doing it again now. Whenever things get too good or a little too close for comfort, you bolt.'

'We both agreed to end it back then,' he bit out, hating how close to the truth she really was and not willing to have this conversation, not here, not now, not ever.

She rolled her eyes. 'Yeah, but you started withdrawing the minute I popped the question. I know, I know, SEALs aren't around much, are in danger constantly, et cetera…et cetera…et cetera… I bought your excuses because I was young and naïve and wanted to make a name for myself just as much as you did, but you know what? This time was different. I wanted to see you again. I wanted to see if we still had sparks. I wanted…'

She trailed off and dropped her gaze, her hands clenched so tightly he could see her knuckles standing out.

'What?'

He fisted his own hands to stop from reaching out to tilt her chin up, to make her meet his gaze. He couldn't touch her. It would undo him completely.

'Never mind.'

He barely heard her whispered words as his mobile phone rang, breaking the escalating tension, and he cursed the bad timing.

The news from the end of the line added to his all-round bad day and he grunted his responses, snapping the phone shut before thrusting it back into his pocket.

'This is getting us nowhere,' he said, eager to escape before the wall around his heart crumbled and left him more vulnerable to this woman than ever. 'I have to go.'

He could've sworn he glimpsed the sheen of tears in her eyes as she nodded and turned away.

'You do what you have to do,' she said, her voice tight and high and totally unnatural.

Despite his anger, his bitterness at himself for letting him get this attached, he wanted to give her some small comfort before walking out of her life for good.

'I just got a transfer. I really do have to go.'

It was totally untrue but maybe this way she'd remember him for doing what he always did—putting his career first—rather than running away because of how deeply she affected him.

In reality, his medical results were ready, and he needed time to prepare himself to hear them before he went for his physical. Meanwhile his heart still reeled from the fact he had no future with Kate.

Sending her a brief salute, he slid behind the wheel of his car and gunned the engine, deliberately not looking back.

Kate watched Ty drive away, tears spilling over and rolling down her cheeks. Angry tears, frustrated tears, useless tears she swiped away while silently chastising herself for being a fool.

She'd had an inkling he'd run to the orphanage, the only place he'd ever called home, after their confrontation and now as she cried enough tears to fill the Mojave desert she wondered if she should've done more to convince him to stay.

However, the second he'd mentioned the transfer she'd known the score. He was running back to his precious SEALs as always, just as he'd said at the start, and nothing she could say or do would change his mind.

'Would you like to come in?'

She turned towards the soft, tentative voice, the concerned

look in Mary's eyes reaching out and drawing her in till all she wanted to do was bawl again.

'Thanks.'

She wiped the tears away with the back of her hand, knowing she must look a fright but not giving a damn, and followed Mary into the kitchen, once again marvelling at her petite stature. No wonder Ty loved her—her fragility just screamed 'pick me up and cherish me'. Even as a woman, Kate almost felt compelled to protect her.

'Would you like a drink?'

'Coffee would be great.'

Kate looked around the kitchen, noting the homely touches that Mary must have instituted to help the orphans feel welcome: the mismatched plates on the dresser, the monstrous cake tin in the shape of Mickey Mouse, the bright mugs arranged in delightful disarray. The last time she'd been here she'd been less observant, too busy watching Ty's reaction to Mary.

Mary placed a mug of steaming coffee in front of her in record time and took a seat opposite.

'You're not having anything?' Kate gestured to the empty table in front of the other woman.

'No. I just had a cup of tea…' Mary trailed off, looking as if she'd made the biggest gaff of all time.

'With Ty?' Kate asked, knowing the answer and wondering why she'd asked the question.

Mary nodded. 'Tell me to butt out if you like, but what's going on with you two?'

Kate wanted to confide in the other woman. Hell, she needed to talk to somebody at this stage. But how could she talk about her feelings for Ty with a woman she hardly knew?

'You can talk to me. Though I love him dearly I won't tell him we spoke.'

Something shrivelled up and died inside Kate. Mary had just confirmed what she'd only suspected to this point.

'Don't you hate me?' Kate asked, admiring Mary for maintaining such a cool façade in the face of her would-be opposition.

Mary looked startled. 'Hate you? Why?'

'For loving Ty.'

There, she'd said the words and they sounded so much more pitiful than when she thought them.

'So you do love him?'

Kate didn't understand the satisfied smirk on Mary's face. She'd expected unsheathed claws, not a knowing grin. 'Yeah, not that it's done me much good.'

'It's not too late,' Mary said, a conspiratorial gleam in her eyes.

As dusk descended the kitchen took on a surreal glow and for a moment Kate thought she'd been trapped in a time warp, having a conversation that didn't make any sense. 'What are you talking about?'

'Go after him. Tell him how you feel.'

Kate was seriously starting to doubt the other woman's sanity; must be all that time spent talking to kids. 'But what about you?'

'Me?' Mary's eyebrows shot heavenward. 'Tyler won't mind. He's used to me interfering in his life.'

'Don't you love him?' Kate asked the redundant question again, her mind a mass of whirling confusion.

Mary's eyes brightened as if a light switch had been turned on. 'Of course I do.'

She paused and Kate's heart sank. 'As a *brother*.'

Ty had said as much and though Kate had believed him she'd thought Mary might have harboured feelings for him. Her memory replayed the way she'd seen Ty and Mary interact and admittedly there had been nothing sexual in it, yet she'd read more into their teasing because of her own in-securities. Yet another blunder in her disastrous week.

'I thought you might have feelings for Ty.'

'God, no!' Mary's vehemence lightened the mood. 'So are you going after him?'

'I can't. He doesn't love me. I tried to talk to him out there but he couldn't wait to get away.'

His image rose before her, the quickly masked hurt in his eyes when she'd accused him of running away.

She'd wanted to shock him, to make him react, anything to get him to look at her with some emotion in his eyes rather than cool control. Instead, it had only served to drive him further away.

'I think Tyler feels a lot more for you than he's letting on.'

A spark of hope flared within Kate. 'Did he say something to you?'

'Just that you were lovers.'

Mary's response quickly doused the spark that had threatened to combust into a bonfire with the right encouragement and her face fell. 'Sex isn't the same as love.'

'I know that and so does Tyler.'

'I don't have any siblings but I know for a fact that if I had a brother I wouldn't be discussing my sex life with him.'

'I know Tyler. He's not that type of guy.'

Kate admired Mary's loyalty but thought her adamant stance in this case was misplaced. 'Did he tell you we were once involved? Engaged?'

'Engaged?' Mary leaned forward, shock written all over her face. 'Are you serious?'

'Guess you didn't know.'

'Tyler mentioned he had a special woman in his life about six years ago but it didn't work out. I haven't seen him date anyone seriously since and I used to rib him about it all the time. That was you?'

Kate nodded, not feeling very special at the moment and wishing things could've been different. 'Uh-huh.'

'So you're the one…'

'The one?'

Suddenly, Kate wished she'd stuck around to face Ty when he'd returned from his first mission. After he'd left she'd thrown herself into her own job, determined to make it to the top. Ironically, she was almost there now and it didn't hold half the appeal it had when she'd been young and ambitious.

'I remember him being pretty cut up at the time and I've never seen him like that again. Till now.'

The impact of Mary's statement took a second to sink in.

'I know he cared about me back then. We both cared. But none of that matters any more because I asked him to stay and he said no. He probably thinks I'm still hung up over my job.'

'Well, are you?'

'No. Sure, I love my job. It's about all I had till Ty walked into my life again.'

'Then tell him.'

Kate shook her head. 'I tried but he didn't want to hear it.'

Mary winced. 'What is it with guys?'

'I don't know. The one I love doesn't want to have anything to do with me.'

'Try bringing them home to twenty kids and see how long they stick around.'

Kate admired Mary for her self-sacrifice but didn't understand it. 'Why do you do it? Look after the kids, I mean.'

'It's my way of giving something back to this place. If my mother hadn't dumped me on the doorstep here after I was born who knows where I might've ended up? Helping out is a small price to pay in return for being raised here.'

Mary's face glowed while she spoke about the orphanage and suddenly Kate wished she could do more than just write the article.

'Ty feels the same way too, doesn't he? That's why he wants to save this place so badly.'

'Yeah, though he's also fixated on a promise he made me when we were teenagers. He said that he'd get us both out of here, to make a life for ourselves. He did it, I didn't and that makes him feel guilty. What he doesn't realise is how much I love working here. I wouldn't do it if I didn't. Besides, it's giving me a good grounding in what I ultimately want to do, which is social work.'

Kate's admiration kicked up another notch. They should rename the orphanage 'Saint Mary's'.

'That's great. Don't worry about Ty. He's out to save the world and everybody in it.'

'And isn't that one of the things you love about him?'

Great, Mary had a talent for reading minds just like Ty.

'You're right.' Kate thought there were a lot of things she loved about him and he would never know.

'Which brings me back to my first point. Go after him. Tell him how you feel. What have you got to lose?'

Everything.

Though she didn't say it, that one word scared her more than anything else.

'He's being transferred. What good would it do?'

Unless she wanted to follow him to the ends of the earth, which she didn't, there was little use in declaring her love. Her knight would ride off into the sunset just as he'd planned. Why did the ending of her fairy tale always suck?

'Make him change his mind.'

Kate stared at Mary in horror. 'And make him hate me for the rest of his life because I made him choose between me and his career? No way.'

'Then go with him,' Mary said, as if it were the easiest thing in the world.

'You think?'

'Why not? If it's happily ever after you want, go for it.'

Kate needed to make a cool, calm, rational decision, not some spur-of-the-moment one based on a love that was probably one-sided, and having Saint Mary egg her on wasn't helping.

'He could be going as far away as Timbuktu,' she muttered, totally floored she could even consider giving up everything for a man who still might walk away any time he fancied, just as he'd already told her many moons ago.

Mary stood up. 'Look, I'm sorry to end our chat but I've got to organise the children's dinner. Think about what I've said. Life's too short not to take chances.' She squeezed Kate's arm as she walked to the stove. 'You owe it to yourselves to try and make this work.'

Kate stared at her, amazed at the camaraderie that had sprung up between them and feeling suitably chastened for all the nasty thoughts she'd harboured.

'Thanks for the coffee and the chat.' She paused for a moment, struggling to find the right words. 'I owe you one.'

Mary smiled. 'Just run the article on this place to keep the doors open. Then we'll be even.'

Kate snapped her fingers. 'The article! I needed to get some info from you. Do you mind if I come back tomorrow?'

'Sure. Maybe you'll have come to a decision by then?' Mary's eyes twinkled and Kate had a feeling they would become firm friends regardless of the outcome of her relationship with Tyler.

'Let me sleep on it.'

Kate knew, though, no matter how many hours she took to dwell on the matter, there were no easy solutions when it came to sorting out the mess with Ty.

Then again, since when had she ever settled for easy?

CHAPTER THIRTEEN

IT HAD been a long couple of days for Tyler. First walking away from Kate and then learning just how badly his knee had deteriorated, then waiting for the physical that could change his life one way or the other.

The docs had given him the usual spiel about success rates and percentages of post-op knees, but in his case they hadn't been encouraging. The cartilage had worn down to the bone and it would take a minor miracle for him to stay in the Navy.

Facing the fact he'd probably never be part of his beloved SEALs again wouldn't be so bad if he could get his head around what had happened with Kate.

What happened to his last fling at fun before he made any life-changing decisions? He'd been determined to hold her at arm's length, flirt with her, have some fun, and enjoy her stimulating company before exiting her life.

Instead, it had blown up in his face like some undetonated bomb and the fallout was just as damaging. He couldn't eat or sleep, her image haunting his mind, and when he did manage to block her out he'd turn a corner and see something to remind him of her.

Take today, for instance. He'd walked past a news-stand and seen the latest edition of *Femme* sitting there. He'd averted his eyes but it was too late and before he knew what was happening he'd bought a copy. Totally sick. He'd never bought a glossy magazine in his life so what was he doing with one lying on his coffee-table now?

The guys on the team were right. Love was a bitch. And now he knew it firsthand.

He glared at the magazine as if it were a venomous snake about to strike. However, the longer he avoided the inevitable, the more he wanted to do it.

Finally, he pulled the tab on a soda, sat down and picked it up. He'd never understood women's obsession for magazines; give him a good thriller novel any day. He flicked open the cover and turned the pages, paying scant attention to the advertisements for make-up and perfume.

There it was. Page nine.

Some of the tension he'd been holding in his gut slowly unwound as he stared at the larger-than-life photo of Mary and the kids at the orphanage.

So Kate had done it.

He read the short piece advertising the upcoming article on the orphanage in next week's issue, complete with address, phone number and web site for donations. As for the feature on the two of them and the auction, he skimmed over it, trying not to notice how she'd blended the skilful words perfectly, outlining the reason behind the man auction, his role in the Navy, painting an accurate and heart-rending picture of the place he'd once called home, the story far surpassing his expectations, and for one second he glowed with pride.

The woman he loved had done this.

Then reality set in.

He tossed the magazine onto the table, tired of rehashing the same old thoughts in his head. Kate was history and the sooner he realised it, the better. Focussing on his physical, adjusting to life as a civilian and finding a new career would be a huge challenge and healthier than pining for a woman he couldn't have.

Padding into the bedroom, he packed his kit, mentally ticking off items as he followed the method he'd used since joining the Navy. Just as he zipped up the first bag he heard a knock on the door, knowing it had to be one of the boys.

'If you've come to give me grief, Bear, save it…' He trailed off as he opened the door to find Kate standing there with a small suitcase in hand.

'Can I come in?'

'Sure.'

He swung the door wider and took a step back, not wanting to brush up against her as she walked in for fear of touching her and finding he couldn't stop.

He needn't have bothered as her signature gardenia fragrance wafted over him and created havoc with his senses as surely and swiftly as her touch would have.

'What are you doing here?'

He gestured to a chair, studiously avoiding looking at her suitcase and what it might imply.

She didn't answer his question. Instead, she placed the suitcase on the floor, picked up the magazine and flipped it open. 'Did you like the article?'

'Yeah, and it looks like the follow-up on the orphanage in the next issue is going to be a winner.'

She shrugged and he watched the way her green ribbed top rode higher to display a tantalising glimpse of tanned, flat stomach beneath and it took all his will-power not to cross the room and haul her into his arms.

'I did what I had to.'

The unreadable expression in her eyes gave him little clue to why she was here though he wished she would stop staring at him as if he'd grown two heads.

Swallowing, he turned away and walked into the kitchen.

'Can I get you anything?' He opened the refrigerator. 'I've got beer, beer and beer.'

When she didn't respond, he looked up and almost jumped; she'd snuck up on him, moving with the stealth of one of his recruits.

'Can we talk?'

The beseeching look in her eyes had him backing away before he knew what he was doing.

'Haven't we said enough?'

He filled the sink, reaching for a pile of dirty plates. In fact, reaching for anything concrete that would keep his hands occupied and away from giving in to their first instinct to touch her.

'I don't think so.'

Her calm voice contrasted with her fiddling hands, which were busily tidying the mail he'd left strewn across the kitchen-top.

'Yeah?' He scrubbed the dishes with particular ferocity before stacking them to dry.

'At least hear me out.'

He glanced over his shoulder, noting her downcast eyes, her wobbly bottom lip. Hell, if she cried he'd never be able to resist taking her into his arms. Emptying the sink in record time, he dried his hands and pointed to the living room. 'We can talk in there.'

She nodded and he resisted the urge to pull her pony-tail as it bobbed. He liked her hair up like that; she looked like a teenager, almost like when he'd first met her. Damn, so much had happened since then.

He waited till she sat down and chose the chair opposite. No use in getting too close.

Kate took a deep breath and plunged straight into her speech before she lost her nerve. 'First up, I'd like to apologise for what I said about you, about running away all the time. I was way out of line.'

'You don't have to do this.'

He stared at her, those familiar blue eyes boring directly into her soul, a place that was empty without him in her life.

'Yeah, I do.'

He shook his head, his too-kissable lips compressed in a hard line. 'Whatever you say won't change facts. We're over. You've got your whole life in front of you. Make the most of it. Move on. Be happy.'

'Not without you,' she murmured, convinced that her thudding heart would drown out her words.

She didn't want to move on. She'd been wrong to agree to only a week, to close the book on their story. From where she stood they had a whole lot of chapters left and she'd have her happily ever after if it killed her.

'I can't give you what you want. We've already discussed this.'

He leaned forward, rested his elbows on his knees and dropped his head into his hands, not looking at her.

She allowed herself the luxury of scanning his bare legs, noting the lean muscles and imagining how they would feel under her hands again. She loved him in shorts. She loved him in anything. She loved him, period. Now all she had to do was convince him of the fact.

'And you still think you can't give me what I need?'

He shrugged, his casualness cutting her to the core. 'I'm sure there are any number of guys just waiting to give you what you need.'

'What do *you* need, Ty?'

He glanced up, his solemn gaze locking with hers across the room, and for one brief second she thought he'd say the word she wanted to hear.

You.

She wanted him to say how much he needed her, how much he loved her despite all that had happened between them, despite the wasted years apart.

But he didn't speak. He just sat there, staring at her with that serious look, not blinking, not flinching, and showing no emotion whatsoever.

Tell him you love him.

Instead, she did the one thing guaranteed to capture his attention, to get some sort of a reaction out of him.

'Well, if you won't tell me what you need, how about I show you?'

Mustering the last of her fleeting courage, she stood up, pulled her top off and shimmied out of her skirt.

No more playing it safe. She would take control, show him what he was missing out on and convince him that they needed each other. For ever.

Tyler's eyes bulged. He couldn't believe that Kate was standing in his living room wearing the sexiest, briefest scraps of lace he'd ever seen. Though what impressed him more were the tempting curves that filled the lingerie and his hands just itched to free them.

'Someone's been to Victoria's Secret.'

It sounded stupid but he had to play it cool till he figured out what the hell he was going to do.

'So what do you think?'

'Nice lace.'

He almost salivated at the thought of peeling the scraps of material away, leaving her creamy skin exposed.

'What about what's inside the lace?'

Her hands slithered down her body and she started playing with the elastic of her panties, driving him insane in the process.

'You'll have to show me.' He forced himself to sit still, wondering if she would take up the challenge.

She did and notched up the level of torture she was inflicting to unbearable.

He watched her push the panties down, step out of them and kick them away. They landed on the coffee-table with a soft plop, pooling in a tempting little heap of black lace, and her bra followed suit as she unhooked it, slipped out of it and threw it at him.

'Great catch,' she said, her husky voice filling the room with promise as he reflexively caught it.

'So, what's the verdict?'

She stood in front of him, wearing nothing but a coy smile.

'Better than the lace. Much better,' he growled as he leaped off the sofa and reached for her.

This was not a good idea.

They were finished and this wouldn't change a thing. He should push her away, send her packing and remember every reason why he had to walk away from the best thing to ever happen to him—while he could still walk.

Closing his eyes, he prayed for control as she moved towards him, driving him to the brink of losing it. Every thought he'd ever had about keeping his distance from her, about walking away and not looking back, almost flew straight out the window as she touched him.

'No.'

He pulled away, his breathing ragged as he marched to the other side of the room, putting some valuable space between them.

He didn't know what had possessed her to come here like this, but he knew that whatever happened he would never forget the sight of his beautiful Katie standing before him wearing nothing but a smile.

As she stared at him the uncertainty in her hazel eyes tore him apart and he gritted his teeth, knowing this final goodbye would be the hardest mission he'd ever faced in his life.

'I think you should get dressed.'

Kate closed her eyes, drowning in mortification. She'd never stripped for him before and strangely hadn't felt self-conscious with the appreciation evident in his eyes as he'd watched her.

However, her act hadn't had the desired effect. Instead of reaching for her and offering her a one-way ticket to wherever he was being transferred he kept his hands firmly planted to his sides while she stood there like a fool in her birthday suit.

She'd taken control hoping to show him what he was missing out on and what had he done? Rejected her touch, put space between them and told her to cover up.

So much for knocking him dead with her body. She would've done better knocking some sense into her head by bashing it against the wall.

Silence engulfed them as she picked up her clothes, trying to muster whatever dignity she could—which wasn't much considering she was stark naked.

'You can get dressed through there.'

He pointed towards the bedroom and walked into the kitchen without a backward glance, leaving her mortified and more alone than she'd ever felt in her entire life.

Struggling to hold back tears, she stumbled towards the bedroom. She couldn't help but notice the two bags lying on his bed, one neatly zipped, the other packed to overflowing. Glancing around the bare, stripped room, she suddenly had her answer.

Nothing she could do or say would change Ty's mind, no words of love, no demonstration of it.

Love might have temporarily blinded her, but the blinkers had well and truly come off now.

Ty didn't want her no matter how much she was willing to give him.

He was ready to move on and who was she to stop him?

CHAPTER FOURTEEN

ONCE she'd dressed and composed herself Kate walked into the living room. Ty looked up from the magazine he held, though she knew he hadn't been looking at it unless his skills extended to reading upside down.

Good. She hoped he felt as rattled as she did.

'When do you leave?' Her voice stayed remarkably steady for a woman who was falling apart inside.

'Tomorrow morning.' He looked at her without quite meeting her eyes.

'You never mentioned where you were going.'

'It's not important.'

Not important? He was walking out of her life for good come tomorrow morning and he didn't want her to know where he was going? Guess it wouldn't be important if he didn't care about her and if his actions weren't enough to convince her of that sad fact, his callous words were.

'A mystery destination? In that case, I don't think I'll be dropping in if I'm ever in the area.'

She forced a smile, knowing her attempt at humour sounded pathetic but grasping at anything to hide her humiliation. And her breaking heart.

'You take care.' He stood up and walked towards her, sending her pulse skittering into overdrive.

'You too.'

Though her mind willed her legs to move, to get out with what little dignity she had left, the message didn't get through. The bleak expression in his eyes jammed all her circuits, rooting her to the spot.

She held her breath as he brushed her cheek with the back of his hand.

'You better go,' he said softly, cupping her chin in his hands, scanning her face with an intensity that suggested he was trying to imprint every last detail into his memory bank.

He leaned towards her and she placed a hand on his chest to stop him, feeling his heat through the cotton and wondering how she could ever live without him again, touching him, smelling him, loving him.

'Don't kiss me, Ty. This is hard enough as it is.'

'Okay.' He sounded shaky and for the first time she thought he might actually care more than he let on.

She picked up her suitcase and walked towards the door, steeling herself not to look back.

'What's the suitcase for?'

She didn't break stride. 'I thought I might be going away but I've changed my mind.'

Or in reality he'd changed it for her the minute he'd shattered her heart by rebuffing her last attempt at making him see they belonged together, and as she pulled the door shut behind her the decisive click rammed home the fact she would never see Ty again.

Striding to the car, she kept her emotions in check till she'd reached its confines, swearing this was the last time she would ever cry over Tyler James.

Tyler watched Kate walk down the path, get into her car and drive away.

Out of his life.

For good.

He should be thankful that he'd had one last glimpse of the best thing that had ever happened to him.

The best thing?

Hell, he'd always been prone to understatement. Kate stimulated him on every level: he admired her drive, her ambition, her zest for life. And as for their physical compatibility—no, he wouldn't let his mind drift off on that tangent.

He needed to think straight, at least for the next few minutes. Something she'd said niggled at his brain and he couldn't quite remember. Was it from before her hot striptease act had driven every sensible thought out of his head?

Every way he looked at it, every angle analysed, all things considered, she was right for him in every way.

Yet he couldn't have her.

Suddenly, it hit him. The suitcase. She'd muttered something about going away and changing her mind. Why would she arrive on his doorstep with a suitcase unless she'd planned on going away with *him*?

Once the wheels started turning his mind shifted into overdrive. If she'd been prepared to go away with him that probably meant she'd put her job on hold. And if Kate had been willing to put her prized promotion on hold to follow him to wherever his fictitious transfer was that meant she loved him more than anything. It was the only answer that made any sense.

Mentally kicking himself and cursing profusely, he grabbed his keys and mobile phone before heading out the door.

His instincts had never let him down before. Maybe it was time he trusted them again, starting with a very important phone call to his commanding officer and the doc.

* * *

Kate needed to get away. Immediately. She couldn't function, let alone think.

So her plan to follow Ty to the ends of the earth hadn't worked out. So what? She could still use the time off.

Hadn't worked out? Not only had her plans backfired, but she'd made an idiot of herself in the process.

Lord, what must Ty think of her? His last impression would be of a woman who was quite happy to come into a guy's house the day before he left town, strip off, offer him her body on a plate and walk away.

'Real classy,' she muttered as she pulled into the LAX car park.

Grabbing her suitcase, she stabbed at the car remote and headed into the departure terminal. She'd been thinking about this for a while and Ty's reappearance in her life had prompted her to seriously reconsider her priorities.

She hadn't been back to Australia in years and what better place to mend a broken heart than home?

Besides, she hadn't spoken to her mum in ages and, though they'd never been close, if there was ever a time she needed a mother now was it.

Before she could chicken out she walked up to the nearest counter and booked a seat on the next flight to Sydney. Doris didn't usually like surprises yet Kate hoped she wouldn't mind this one.

Finding the nearest payphone, she placed a call to work, notifying them of her change of plans. Henry had thought she'd been crazy taking a month off as he was about to announce her promotion, but she'd convinced him that a little 'R and R' was in order, especially after she'd come through for the magazine.

Luckily she hadn't thrown in her job as her first impulse had been to do. Sure, she'd been ready to follow Ty anywhere, but had wisely decided to test the waters of their relationship first before doing anything as drastic as leaving *Femme*. Who knew, maybe she'd jeopardised her chances at the promotion anyway as Henry didn't take kindly to 'flighty' females.

She abhorred his outdated views, but it had never affected her and she'd played his game to ensure her precious job was safe.

Not that it mattered any more. Nothing did. If she didn't have Ty in her life everything else just wasn't enough.

Once she boarded the plane and it took off she snoozed, eager to catch up on some of the sleep she'd been missing the last week. When Ty hadn't been there in the flesh he'd haunted her restless dreams, making any type of rest impossible. Hopefully, the soothing sound of the ocean at Bondi would lull her to sleep for the next few weeks. She needed all the help she could get.

It seemed as if she'd barely closed her eyes before a flight attendant shook her awake, requesting that she return her seat to the upright position for landing. Glancing out the window, she watched the sparkling Sydney city lights reflect off the harbour, the impressive Harbour Bridge and Opera House clearly visible.

It had been six years since she'd seen her home city and now she was here her stomach churned with excitement. Though she adored LA she knew exactly how Dorothy had felt landing back in Kansas: there was no place like home.

After checking into a boutique hotel in Bondi almost metres from her old home she freshened up and headed out, determined to ignore the possibility of jet lag and eager to see everything her old suburb had to offer.

As she strolled along the teeming streets filled with trendy boutiques and vibrant cafés the tension of the last week slowly slipped away. So much had changed here yet the familiar scents of sea air, fish and chips and lattes infused her with a calm she hadn't felt since she'd first seen Ty's name on that damn auction list.

A couple of weeks here would be good for her. Sydney was as far away from LA and Ty as she could get and the perfect place to deal with her memories and move on.

Speaking of memories…she found her feet unconsciously treading the well-worn path to her old home and, though she wasn't ready to face her mum just yet—another few days should psyche her up for that auspicious occasion—she stopped outside the house, hiding like a fugitive behind an old oak on the opposite side of the street.

Narrowing her eyes, she peered across the street, more than a little surprised at the changes wrought: box hedges perfectly trimmed, terracotta pots filled with palms flanking a new leadlight door, an ornate porch light switched on. The house looked welcoming, in stark contract to her memories of it being a prison as she trudged up the same path every day after school and later after her internship at *The Sydney Morning Herald.*

She'd hated this house, hated the fact her father had abandoned her here and left her with a mother who obviously resented her as a constant reminder of the man who had messed up her life.

But maybe that wasn't true. Now that she'd loved and lost herself, maybe her mum had been doing the best she could while trying to mend her broken heart and raise a curious kid at the same time.

And she'd been curious, always asking questions about her father, about America where he came from, practically rubbing her mum's nose in it. It hadn't been intentional, but in hindsight she was surprised her mum hadn't told her to shut up rather than answering her questions with pursed lips and a disapproving frown.

She'd blamed her mum for a lot back then, convincing herself that her mother's parenting had made her the way she was: desperate to escape, happy to travel halfway across the world to do so and silly enough to fall for the first guy to look her way.

Pretty ridiculous, considering her mother hadn't made the decision to leave home, fall for a guy in record time and want to marry him. She'd done that of her own accord, made her own decisions, and it was time to recognise her mistakes, accept it and move on. Without acknowledging the truth she'd never be able to let go and stop loving Ty.

Time to put the past to rest and face the future, in all aspects of her life.

Turning away, she headed back to the hotel.

Maybe it was jet lag catching up with her, maybe the sentimentality of being back in Bondi, maybe the realisation that Ty truly was her past, but whatever it was she had the distinct craving for a long, hot bubble bath followed by several mind-numbing daiquiri chasers.

Tyler was a man of action who hated procrastination in any form so when he made up his mind to do something it had to happen—like yesterday.

However, pursuing Kate took time: he spoke to his doc to push back the date and details for his physical, and he survived his commander's bawling out for requesting extra leave before focussing his attention on the main goal.

Convincing Kate that he was the man for her despite everything he'd said and done to the contrary.

However, when he arrived on her doorstep pride in hand he discovered she'd gone away. That seriously dented his confidence. Perhaps she had been going away when she'd dropped in on him? Or worse, perhaps he'd read a lot more into this than he should have?

Doubts plagued him before his resolve settled. Whatever her motives, he knew what he had to do. If he could find her, that was.

He contacted her office and spoke to Di, her assistant. Their conversation was short and sweet. If he'd thought his commander had been tough he'd been dreaming. Di gave him a tongue-lashing for what he'd apparently done to her best friend before dropping the vital piece of information he'd been after: Kate had taken off to Sydney for a little R and R.

That threw him.

Either she'd planned to go to Sydney all along or she'd run away, as far from him as possible.

There was only one way to find out.

CHAPTER FIFTEEN

FOR a born and bred Sydney girl it was only natural Kate loved the beach so she found herself attending a twilight surf carnival on her second night in Bondi. Nothing like the sight of a few half-naked bronzed Aussie guys to take her mind off her troubles.

Plonking down on the sand, she sipped her take-out latte while listening to the pop-cum-reggae of a local band, content to people watch.

Kids squealed with delight, splashing each other in the shallows while teenagers strolled hand in hand along the water's edge. Tourists posed for photos with surf life-savers while a busker imitated a robot on speed, but it was the cosy couples that eventually got to her with their locked gazes, tight clinches and inane smiles.

Finishing her latte in record time, she dumped the cup in a bin and headed up the beach, hoping a quick stroll would clear her head.

The waves broke around her ankles in swirling foam as she wandered along the water's edge, leaving the carnival revellers far behind, trying not to think past the serene beauty of a balmy Sydney evening.

'Excuse me. Could you give me a hand? I seem to have lost my way.'

Her feet froze, sinking into the soft sand as she turned slowly, wondering if she'd drunk one too many daiquiris before dinner.

'Think you can help a sailor with a lousy sense of direction?'

Her heart pounded as she stared at Ty, watching his lips move and hearing the words but not quite believing he was real as her gaze drifted to the yellow board-shorts, Hawaiian shirt and striped surf cap he wore.

'Not to mention lousy dress sense.'

The man of her dreams was standing less than two feet away on Bondi beach and that was all she could say?

Way to go, Kate.

He stared at her, his gaze dropping to her waist. 'Yeah, well, at least I'm not wearing the local vegetation.'

She noted the appreciative gleam in his eyes and her body responded in predictable fashion, a deep, burning heat spreading through every muscle and bone, melting her brain in the process. The carnival had a luau theme so she'd worn a grass skirt at the insistence of the hotel concierge to join in the fun. However, right now the fronds tickling her legs made her feel downright naked.

'Though what I wouldn't give for a lawnmower right now…' He trailed off, the intensity of his stare leaving little doubt in her mind as to what would happen to her skirt if he had one.

'There's a law against destruction of the local flora,' she said, wondering what the heck he was doing here while fighting the urge to fling herself into his arms.

He raised an eyebrow. 'Who said anything about destruction? I'd merely cut back a bit to display the beauty underneath.'

She tried to ignore the glow that blossomed at his words. Nothing had changed. After all that had happened between them, here they were exchanging quips as they always did.

'What are you doing here?'

She cut to the chase, afraid that if they continued their

banter she'd do something stupid like beg him to give them a second chance. Now that would be stupid, considering she'd already tried and he'd ended it anyway.

'I came to see you.'

She folded her arms and tried to focus on the reason she was here, to get away from the man standing in front of her, acting as if nothing had happened. 'Why?'

The darkness hid the expression in his eyes. 'I have an assignment for you.'

Disappointment flooded her. So what had she been expecting?

A declaration of undying love? As if.

'Can't help you. I'm taking a break from work.'

He flashed the familiar killer smile, the one that made her knees shake. 'I'd make it worth your while.'

If he expected her to melt at the sight of his pearly whites, he had another thing coming. Steeling her traitorous body against reacting further, she shook her head.

'Sorry. Not interested.'

He reached out, running the back of his hand down her cheek. 'Don't you want to hear what it's about?'

Her resolve unravelled in an instant as her skin tingled from his brief touch.

'No.'

She held her breath as his fingers trailed along her jaw-line before cupping her chin and tilting her head up.

He stared into her eyes and all the feelings she'd managed to suppress the last few days flooded back, rendering her helpless.

'I have a friend who needs help. He just made a really bad decision about a woman he's crazy about and is feeling a tad uncertain about what he should do next. What do you think he should do?'

Her pulse raced as his thumb reached up and stroked her bottom lip, sending excited shivers skittering down her spine.

'Depends how crazy he is over the woman,' she managed to say, quelling the urge to nip at his thumb.

'He's totally loco. Stark raving mad. Can't eat, can't sleep.'

'Sounds bad.'

Her breath hitched as his thumb slid perilously close to her mouth for a second and she knew in an instant that she'd stepped right back on their personal roller coaster and couldn't do a damn thing about it.

His eyes widened as he continued in a husky voice. 'Should he tell the woman how he feels?'

Kate took a step back, breaking the contact between them. The ride was rocky enough without their ever-present, all-consuming physical attraction wreaking havoc with her senses. She couldn't think straight when he touched her.

'Sure. Why not take a chance? What does he have to lose?'

'His mind. His sanity. His heart.'

Their gazes locked and held as silence enveloped them, heavy with expectation and untold truths.

Tyler took a deep breath and exhaled slowly. Nothing had prepared him for this. He'd trained for every eventuality in his job, had accepted his diagnosis from the docs, yet felt powerless when pinned beneath the stare of the woman he loved. It totally unnerved him.

He'd been mad to follow her out here.

Why couldn't he have waited till tomorrow when they could have met in the safety of a hotel bar? Instead, he'd called in favours from an Aussie commander he'd met once to locate her hotel, then, having spotted her walking away from the carnival near the hotel, he'd been stupid enough to follow her onto a deserted section of the beach, lured by a glimpse of her sexy legs beneath the ridiculous grass skirt and the promise of more delights underneath.

He shouldn't have touched her. As soon as he'd caressed her skin, all logic had fled and he'd been instantly ruled by his anatomy rather than his brain. Rather than stating the truth from the start he'd resorted to some childish word game, knowing she would see right through him, and now he waited like a condemned man praying for a pardon.

When she finally spoke, he almost shouted, 'Get it over and done with.' Instead, she fixed him with that tell-tale glare.

'Are you saying he loves her?'

'Yeah.'

The noose slipped around his neck and tightened. So much for a pardon.

'Enough to give up his transfer? To stick around?'

He heard the incredulity in her voice even though the darkness hid her expression.

'There is no transfer. He hid behind that to avoid telling the truth, which he'll get around to if she gives him another chance. As for sticking around, he'd be in it for the long haul this time, if she is.'

'What do you mean no transfer?'

Taking a deep breath, he launched into the explanation that would make or break them one way or the other.

'This guy has a secret. Several, actually. There is no transfer because he's having a physical soon to determine whether he is still considered fit to serve given the state of his knee. Though he pretty much knows it's the end of the line and the results of the physical will get him booted out of the Navy. He couldn't tell the woman he loves because he didn't want her hanging around him out of pity so he did the only thing he could. He walked away. He'd already made a promise to himself never to have to depend on anyone and, being a big, macho SEAL, he always kept his promises. The only problem with this one, though, was that he hadn't counted on how much he loved this woman.'

He paused, wishing she'd give him some sign of encouragement, some indication she believed him.

'When he returned from his first mission where he couldn't stop thinking about her, he weakened and looked her up, but she'd gone. Which was fair enough, he told himself. They'd both agreed on a split. And after all, a promise is a promise. He's gone through the motions the last six years. And then she shows up just over a week ago around the time he's scheduled to go in for the physical that will probably end his career and rather than push her away he's selfish, takes what he can get for the week, ready to walk away at the end.'

She didn't blink, move a muscle or give him any indication she was listening to any of this but he ploughed on anyway, needing to explain why he'd treated her so badly.

'His plan was working out just fine till she showed up on his doorstep, suitcase in hand, and it wasn't till he'd pushed her away for good this time that he realised what she was trying to do. He thinks this woman loves him, that she was willing to follow him to wherever in order to give them another chance, but he was still too scared. In all probability he won't be anything more than a washed-up ex-sailor in a few weeks; the docs have already more or less confirmed it. Why should a vibrant, beautiful, career woman be stuck in a dead-end relationship with a guy like that? Then it hit him. He owed her the truth if nothing else. He didn't want to face his future, uncertain as it is, without telling her how much she means to him, how much he loves her, how she's the best thing that ever happened to him and that none of this is her fault. It never was.'

Tyler exhaled, a vice-like pain gripping his heart as Kate stepped away, putting more distance between them.

'Tell your *friend* he has a lot of work to do.'

What was that supposed to mean? Did he have a chance or not? Had she heard a word he'd said? Had she absorbed the implications?

She shook her head, a sad expression on her face. 'The

woman he supposedly loves has no idea what goes through this guy's head. He pushed her away years ago and is still pushing. He pushed so hard she gave up. And now he tells her the truth, something he should've done before, and expects her to take him back? What makes him think she'd even consider it?'

'This,' he said, covering the short distance between them in a second and reaching out to her.

His lips crushed hers, stifling any further protest she might make as he claimed her mouth, ravishing her in a long, deep kiss. He'd wanted to do it since the first minute he'd seen her again and, now that he had her in his arms, he didn't want to hold back and sure as hell never wanted to let go.

She squirmed against him as his hands wandered, touching her everywhere. Her silky skin teased his fingertips and he couldn't get enough of her, sliding his hand up her bare thigh, over the curve of her hip, across the smooth expanse of stomach and finally coming to rest, cupping her breast.

'I love it when you wear bikinis,' he murmured.

She leaned back, offering herself to him like a tempting sacrifice for a feasting god. 'Sweet talking won't get you anywhere this time.'

Her fingers wound through his hair, tugging him closer, urging him to taste, to savour. However, he didn't stop there. He rained moist, deep kisses all over her exposed skin, trailing along the tempting hollow at the base of her throat, relishing her delicate skin and the light, salty taste from the sea spray.

'Ty, we're on a beach,' she said, the sinuous writhing of her body belying the conservative logic of her words.

'And there's no one around down here.'

He drew back to look at her, noting her swollen, slick lips and flushed cheeks, highlighted by the soft moonlight.

God, he loved this woman, heart, body and soul. And how did he show it? By pawing her on a public beach?

His conscience told him to pull away, to take it slow and convince her of his feelings, but his body had other ideas.

Kate decided the argument. 'I've missed you,' she whispered against the side of his mouth as she kissed him.

'Same here, kiddo,' he ground out, barely managing to keep from taking her on the spot.

Kate's heart flip-flopped at his smile as her brain warred with her heart. This was crazy. She'd put time and space between them to get over exactly what she was feeling at that moment: floundering, yearning, wanting him more than ever.

'We should stop this,' she said, stepping away from him. 'This isn't supposed to happen.'

He traced her face with his fingertips, skimming her skin in a feather-light touch. 'You're right. I wanted to talk, to try and work things out between us.'

'You really did all this because of some weird promise to yourself?' She whacked him on the chest. 'What were you thinking?'

Wrapping his arms around her, he snuggled her close. 'SEALs are about honour and integrity and loyalty but a promise means more to me. When I was growing up it's all I focussed on. I promised myself I'd get out of the orphanage, I promised to make something of myself and I promised I'd give something back to those who helped me along the way, like Mary. However, I'd been let down by people I'd loved too many times growing up and I made a promise not to depend on anyone, not to get emotionally attached to anyone ever again.'

'So why did you get involved with me back then?'

A slight frown puckered her brow and he resisted the urge to lean down and smooth it with his lips.

Holding her close, he knew he had to make her believe him. 'Because I fell in love with you, because I wanted to build a family with you, a family of my own, a family that I never had. Yeah, it was quick and it took me by surprise, but I'd been virtually alone my whole life, lived by strict rules both at the orphanage and in the Navy, and for once I wanted to make an impulsive decision, one that involved my heart and not my head. Unless you count the fact I lost it over you.'

'Then why did you agree to end it?'

He'd been kicking himself over the very same question for the last six years.

'Because you were young and I didn't want to take advantage of you. Sure, I was crazy about you, head-over-heels crazy, but I knew that first love can fade as quickly as it comes and I wanted to give you time, see if you still felt the same way after you wised up, after I came back from a long absence.'

Her expression softened but she still looked at him with a quizzical look in her eyes. 'Okay, that explains why you quit first time around. Why push me away now?'

'It's the whole washed-up thing. I didn't want you tied down to a guy like that. I *don't* want you tied down to a guy like that, but I had to set the record straight after the way I'd treated you.'

'That's nonsense. You should've asked me what I wanted rather than making decisions for me.'

He captured her face in his hands and stared deeply into her eyes. 'I may end up a grouchy ex-sailor who can barely walk. Do you know what that means?'

The sheen of tears sparkled in the moonlight and he brushed away a lone tear as it trickled down her soft cheek.

'Give me some credit,' she said, turning her cheek to rest it against his hand and gazing up at him with apprehension in her hazel eyes. 'I'm a big girl. I can make my own choices and I know what I want. What do you want?'

'I want to take care of you.'

He spoke so softly, the sound of the waves crashing against the shore almost drowned him out.

'What's that supposed to mean?'

'Damn it, Kate. Do I have to spell it out?'

'Yes, you do.' She barely paused, the words tumbling out in an angry rush. 'After an amazing week you've done everything in your power to push me away even after I hinted at how I feel and asked you to stay. Then you follow me halfway round the world, spin me some story, which I assume is the truth, then skirt around the issue all over again. Don't you get it? I'm in love with you, you moron.'

There, she'd said it and he hadn't moved an inch, not even a flicker of an eyelash.

'Your declaration could do with a little work,' he said, the corners of his mouth twitching as a big, sloppy grin spread across his face.

'I hate you.' She pummelled his chest, her fists barely making a mark before he stilled her wrists.

'No, you don't. You love me as much as I love you.' His grin widened as she stared up at him, speechless. 'What? Nothing to say? That's got to be a first.'

She reached up, cradling his face in her hands as she pulled him towards her.

'Shut up and kiss me,' she said, marvelling that the man of her dreams had finally come to his senses.

'Is that any way to talk to your future husband? But just to let you know, this time I'm doing the asking and, this time, it will be for ever.'

His lips brushing hers saved her from responding. Besides, he knew her answer anyway. She'd always been his from the very first minute they'd battled wills all those years ago.

'You'll always be my Odd Bod, you know. For the rest of your life. Inside and outside the bedroom, for better or worse, and all the rest of that jargon.'

He caressed her cheek, his touch achingly familiar. 'I'm all yours…boss.'

EPILOGUE

'I ALWAYS wanted a beach wedding.'

Kate turned in the circle of Ty's arms and smiled up at her new husband, the clear blue Bondi sky reflected in his beautiful eyes. 'That's because you're obsessed with water. Once a SEAL, always a SEAL.'

Ty shrugged, his broad shoulders tugging at the tux jacket that fitted his body so perfectly. 'Hey, you can take the boy out of the Navy but you can't take the Navy out of the boy.'

Kate's smile waned as she reached up to cup his cheek. 'Do you miss it?'

His blue eyes clouded for a moment, as if lost in some precious memory, before he shook his head and grinned, the same cocky smile that captured her heart so long ago.

'Honestly? I miss the guys, but my new job keeps me too busy to spend much time reminiscing on the good old days.'

Kate kissed him on the lips, soft, lingering, the type of kiss that needed no words, the type of kiss that told him exactly how amazing he was.

'I'm so proud of you. Any other guy would've wallowed in self-pity after your physical didn't pan out a year ago and you had no option but to leave the Navy. But not my guy, uh-uh. Instead, after a painful knee replacement and months of rehab, you throw yourself whole-heartedly into establishing a youth centre at the orphanage and give Mary some much-needed time out to follow her own dreams.'

She sighed, snuggling closer to him. 'That's my guy, just as much of a hero as he ever was running covert ops or bringing in the baddies.'

'You think I'm that good, huh?'

'Oh, yeah,' she said, leaning into him with her hips, loving the naughty gleam in his eyes as her pelvis made contact with his. 'You're very, very good.'

He laughed, a low, intimate rumble of laughter that enveloped her like a warm blanket on a cold night. 'Watch it, Mrs James, or I might decide to skip the reception part and whisk you over those sand dunes to have my wicked way with you.'

'Promises, promises,' she murmured, her hands skimming his back and coming to rest on his butt where she gave a gentle squeeze.

'Hey, you two! Cut it out! Save it for later.'

They laughed and pulled apart, grinning like a couple in love as they turned to see Bear with an equally goofy grin on his face.

'Great timing as always, Bear,' Ty said, slipping an arm around her waist. 'And I'd expect better of you, Mary. You're supposed to be keeping this big lug in line.'

Mary rolled her eyes. 'I have as much chance of keeping him in line as I did with you all those years growing up.'

Kate sent Mary a wink, knowing exactly how demanding living with a big, brawny, alpha guy could be. 'If Bear's as much of a pussycat as Ty, your job must be a piece of cake.'

'Pussycat? *Pussycat?*' Ty's splutter of indignation had them all laughing. 'Did you hear that, Bear? A guy leaves the Navy for two seconds and he's demoted to pussycat status. Man, that sucks.'

Bear shrugged and draped a protective arm across Mary's shoulders, the big guy towering over the petite woman. 'Take it from me, TJ. Never argue with a woman. Works for me.'

Mary elbowed him in the ribs and chuckled at his mock double-over. 'As if.'

Kate smiled and made a T sign with her hands. 'Okay, guys, time out. This is our wedding day. Time to get the party started.'

'Too right,' Bear and Mary said in unison before turning to each other as Bear swung the laughing woman into his arms and planted a huge lip-smacking kiss on her mouth. 'Later, you two.'

Ty shook his head. 'Tell me again why I introduced them.'

'Because you love Mary, you love Bear and they're a match made in heaven.'

'And you're too much of a romantic,' he said, dropping a kiss on her lips before returning his attention to the couple as they sauntered away, arms wrapped tightly around each other's waists. 'Though I have to say I've never seen Mary so happy. She's revelling in the social work course and dotes on Bear. As for him, he deserves his fair share of happiness too considering his heart's as big as the rest of him.'

'My husband, the matchmaker.'

Kate smiled up at him, oblivious to the sun, sand and four-piece jazz band just starting up in a nearby pavilion where a seafood buffet was laid out for them, oblivious to everything but the incredible man staring at her as if she was the best thing he'd ever seen.

The tenderness in his eyes left her breathless as he drew her close again.

'You know, none of this would've happened if you hadn't run that article on the orphanage. Mary would still be trapped there if that international conglomeration hadn't come up with the funds to keep the place open and to hire new staff. So in a way you're the matchmaker, not me.'

'Fine, I'll take all the credit.'

She smiled and traced a lazy finger down his cheek. 'It's great how everything's come full circle, isn't it? We're reunited, you've kept your promise to Mary and you're back at the orphanage doing something you love. Pretty amazing if you ask me.'

'Speaking of full circle…' Ty sent a pointed glance over her right shoulder and she half turned in time to see her mother flash a tentative, shy smile before taking a champagne flute from a passing waiter. 'I think Doris has wanted to talk to you since the ceremony ended but we've been caught up.'

'Nothing wrong with being wrapped up in each other,' Kate said, giving him a quick kiss on the lips before reluctantly slipping out of his embrace. 'But you're right. I need to have a quick chat with Mum before the festivities get under way.'

'Don't be long.'

Ty's subtle tap on her butt, combined with the naughty quirk of his lips, left her in little doubt that her sexy husband wanted her by his side as much as possible, exactly where she wanted to be.

Kate blew him a kiss and headed for her mum, who was looking extremely elegant in a lavender dress that accentuated her figure and took years off her. Kate had always thought of her mum as wearing drab clothes and a perpetual frown, but thankfully those memories had been clouded by Kate's own unhappiness. Now that she'd come to terms with her past, she saw her mum in a whole new light.

'You look great, Mum.'

Kate reached out and laid a hand on her mum's arm, pleased when Doris turned and her face lit up.

'And you make a beautiful bride, dear.'

They hugged and Kate blinked back the sudden sting of tears, thinking of all the years she'd missed this, grateful they'd managed to patch things up despite their time apart.

'You did a great job co-ordinating things from this end, Mum. Organising a Sydney wedding from LA with the deadlines I've had to meet would've been a killer if it hadn't been for you.'

Doris smiled, a glimmer of tears in her eyes. 'It was the

least I could do, after the botched job I did of being a real mum when you were growing up.'

Kate held up her hand. 'Uh-uh, enough. We've been through all that. You were doing the best you could with a broken heart and I was being a selfish brat blaming you for Dad running out on us. It's in the past.'

She smiled and squeezed her mum's hand. 'Besides, look at our futures.'

They turned in unison to see Ty chatting to Percy Robertson, Doris's new partner, a debonair seventy-year-old who doted on her.

'We're so lucky,' Doris said, slipping an arm around Kate's waist and hugging her close.

'We sure are.'

Kate sighed, content to stare at her new husband all day. However, Ty looked up at that exact moment and smiled, the irresistible magnetic pull between them a force even at this distance.

'I'll see you later, Mum.'

Doris laughed. 'If I had a guy look at me like that I'd go running too.'

Kate smiled as she slipped off her sandals and headed in Ty's direction, her gaze fixed on her husband who was already halfway across the sand to meet her.

'I missed you,' he said, capturing her in his arms and taking her breath away with a swift, thorough kiss.

'I missed you too.'

Her heart expanded at the adoration in his eyes, the sexy smile playing about his delicious lips.

'We've waited a long while for this wedding, Katie. Let's go have the time of our lives.'

'I'm with you all the way,' she said, slipping her hand into his, eager to take the first steps towards the rest of their lives, together.

HARLEQUIN *Presents*

HARLEQUIN *Presents*

EXPECTING!

**She's sexy,
successful
and pregnant!**

Relax and enjoy
our fabulous series
about couples whose passion
results in pregnancies…
sometimes unexpected!

Our next arrival will be in April 2008:

ACCIDENTALLY
PREGNANT,
CONVENIENTLY WED

by Sharon Kendrick

Book # 2718

Having been burned badly before, Fleur Stewart wants
to stay away from Spanish billionaire Antonio Rochas.
But Antonio is sexy, smoldering and doesn't intend
to let Fleur go easily….

www.eHarlequin.com

HP12708

REQUEST YOUR
FREE BOOKS!

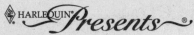 HARLEQUIN® *Presents*~ ®

PASSION GUARANTEED SEDUCTION

2 FREE NOVELS
PLUS 2
FREE GIFTS!

YES! Please send me 2 FREE Harlequin Presents® novels and my 2 FREE gifts (gifts are worth about $10). After receiving them, if I don't wish to receive any more books, I can return the shipping statement marked "cancel". If I don't cancel, I will receive 6 brand-new novels every month and be billed just $4.05 per book in the U.S. or $4.74 per book in Canada, plus 25¢ shipping and handling per book and applicable taxes, if any*. That's a savings of close to 15% off the cover price! I understand that accepting the 2 free books and gifts places me under no obligation to buy anything. I can always return a shipment and cancel at any time. Even if I never buy another book, the two free books and gifts are mine to keep forever.

106 HDN ERRW 306 HDN ERRL

Name _____ (PLEASE PRINT)

Address _____ Apt. #

City _____ State/Prov. _____ Zip/Postal Code

Signature (if under 18, a parent or guardian must sign)

Mail to the **Harlequin Reader Service:**
IN U.S.A.: P.O. Box 1867, Buffalo, NY 14240-1867
IN CANADA: P.O. Box 609, Fort Erie, Ontario L2A 5X3

Not valid to current subscribers of Harlequin Presents books.

Want to try two free books from another line?
Call 1-800-873-8635 or visit www.morefreebooks.com.

* Terms and prices subject to change without notice. N.Y. residents add applicable sales tax. Canadian residents will be charged applicable provincial taxes and GST. This offer is limited to one order per household. All orders subject to approval. Credit or debit balances in a customer's account(s) may be offset by any other outstanding balance owed by or to the customer. Please allow 4 to 6 weeks for delivery. Offer available while quantities last.

Your Privacy: Harlequin Books is committed to protecting your privacy. Our Privacy Policy is available online at www.eHarlequin.com or upon request from the Reader Service. From time to time we make our lists of customers available to reputable third parties who may have a product or service of interest to you. If you would prefer we not share your name and address, please check here. ☐

HP08

I ♥

HARLEQUIN *Presents*

BROUGHT TO YOU BY FANS OF
HARLEQUIN PRESENTS.

We are its editors and authors
and biggest fans—and we'd
love to hear from YOU!

Subscribe today to our online blog at
www.iheartpresents.com

Private jets. Luxury cars. Exclusive five-star hotels.
Designer outfits for every occasion and an entourage
to see to your every whim…

In this brand-new collection,
ordinary women step into the
world of the super-rich and are

TAKEN BY
THE MILLIONAIRE